THE CODE

A Cold War thriller

Nick Elliott

Seaward Publishing

THE CODE

By Nick Elliott
Published by Seaward Publishing
Amazon Edition

ISBN 978-0-9929028-7-2

Formatted by Jo Harrison – Author Assistant

To my granddaughters,

Iona and Laila

'It is insane that two men, sitting on opposite sides of the world, should be able to decide to bring an end to civilisation.'

John F. Kennedy, commenting on the Cuban Missile Crisis, 27 October 1962

'Peace is not the absence of conflict, it is the ability to handle conflict by peaceful means.'

Paraphrased from Ronald Reagan's Address to the Nation on the eve of the Soviet–United States Summit Meeting in Geneva, 14 November 1985

Author's Note

The Code is a prequel to the subsequent Angus McKinnon thrillers: *Sea of Gold*, *Dark Ocean* and *Black Reef*. It spans the period from 1963 up to and including the Millennium.

By way of Kim Philby's infamous treachery and his defection to Moscow, the book follows the espionage career of Valdis, a Latvian merchant marine officer, and his bleak encounter with Angus, which leads to their collaboration and to an enduring friendship. This partnership and the high-risk mission they must pursue together form the basis of the story.

Along the way, Angus himself is introduced to the perilous world of spying, marking his own transition from seafarer to marine investigator, a career move that will invariably entangle him in the murky events of international espionage within the maritime world.

Sharing the same name as Nicholas Elliott, a senior British intelligence officer during the 1950s and '60s, helped spark the initiating idea for the story. I have therefore recreated an approximation of his character under a fictional name.

So *The Code*, at least in its early stages, is a work of reimagined history.

Nick Elliott

Scotland, 2021

Chapter 1

Beirut

23 January 1963

Philby took little heed of the storm that swept across the city that night. His mind was elsewhere. He'd been drinking on and off all day, mostly vodka, but he wasn't drunk. At least, he didn't think he was. To Kim Philby, being drunk was an attitude of mind: something controllable and, not least, a tool of his trade. It had to be. Tonight though, his self-control was on the point of collapse. This was it. His time was up. He'd thought about how it would be for so many years, rehearsed it in his mind yet never quite expected the time would come for the vanishing act, for the fade.

He met his KGB handler on the corner of Rue Kantari, the street where he lived, and May Ziadeh. He wore a Burberry trenchcoat and a black Homburg clamped firmly onto his head. He carried a small, battered leather suitcase, his go bag, containing two shirts, some underwear, socks, a sponge bag and a couple of novels, both of them Russian classics: Dostoyevsky's *Crime and Punishment* and Tolstoy's *The Cossacks*. Any irony in the former's title did not occur to him. He had never considered himself a criminal and did not see his defection now as in any way a punishment. He climbed into the back of the car beside the handler, a burly KGB veteran a few years older than Philby and a man he'd never warmed to. With headlights cutting through the rain, they drove off into the night. The gusts rocked the car as they wound their way through the deserted streets towards Beirut's port, the car's wipers struggling to cope with the rain that lashed the windscreen, the driver hunched over the wheel, gripping it tightly to prevent the car from veering off the road. Winter storms were not unusual in Lebanon but this was a wild one. Philby couldn't help thinking it was a portent.

Only briefly did he think of the dinner party where he'd been expected that evening. And what his wife, Eleanor, would think, if she only knew. Neither did he spare much thought for the past. There'd be time for reflection later – plenty of time. Betrayal of his country, of the Service, or of the men and women whose lives had been lost as a result of his treachery – these things didn't cross his mind for a minute. For what he had done was for a cause. To Philby, that was what counted: the cause of Socialism. For him it was a creed. For the past thirty-odd years he'd fought for that cause as one fought a war. And in war there were casualties, or so he rationalised. But there was more to it than that, though he would never admit it, even to himself. The truth was that he'd become irrationally addicted to the thrill of secrecy and deception. It was a drug, just like the alcohol he consumed so liberally.

He forced the door of the car open, pushing it against the wind. Rain swept sideways across the quayside as the two men struggled to make their way towards the ship. Despite the shelter provided by the breakwaters, white horses rode madly across the harbour and the vessel ranged awkwardly against her fenders. Her name, *Dolmatova*, showed starkly white on black on the prow above them. Philby found the femininity of the name strangely comforting and in doing so, despite himself, was forced to recognise the unfamiliar feeling that had lodged itself in his gut as dread. He'd learned to live with the insecurities of life as a double agent, as the mole, to disguise his inner feelings and control his emotions. He'd become skilled in the art of deception and of manipulating people and situations. And, perhaps because of the gentlemanly culture that pervaded the Service, he had never felt seriously endangered in the physical sense. Now though, control was in the hands of others. He was headed for Moscow. Philby dismissed the anxiety he briefly felt. He had friends in Moscow. He'd served their cause loyally for so long. He would be feted, lionised as a hero.

As he and his stony-faced handler made their way towards the ship, heads bowed against the storm, Philby took little notice of the two men coming down the gangway. The man in front was Valdis Ozols. A Latvian, he was the ship's third mate and, in accordance with common practice, was also the *Dolmatova*'s political officer. Behind him was another Latvian, an able seaman. Though he didn't know it, it was this second man's identity that Philby would assume for the purpose of his onward journey.

Leaning forward against the weather, the two Latvians moved towards the car that had brought Philby and his handler to the ship. The AB got in beside the driver. Valdis Ozols went round to the driver's side and exchanged a few words with him. Stepping back, he paused to look after them as they drove off, then he turned to walk back to the ship.

From the darkness over by one of the cargo warehouses twenty yards away, someone called his name. He stopped and turned in the direction of the voice, not sure whether he'd heard correctly over the sound of the storm. Then a tall figure stepped out of the shadows. 'Come,' he called, beckoning Valdis towards him.

'Who is it?'

'We'd like a word,' called the figure, speaking fluent Russian, a language Valdis understood almost as well as his mother tongue; well enough to tell that it wasn't the mother tongue of the tall, stooped stranger; he was fluent perhaps, but not a native speaker.

Valdis hesitated, more curious than alarmed. The voice was not threatening, rather it was relaxed – a deep, measured tone. He walked cautiously over to where the man was waiting. He'd moved out from the shadows and was standing beside one of the quay cranes concealed from the ship. Now Valdis could make out another man, even taller, behind him. The first man stepped forward, his hand outstretched. 'Pleased to meet you, my dear fellow,' he said, again in his formal Russian, his voice carrying above the wind which whistled through the crane's superstructure. 'Care to join me for a drink?'

The two men shook hands, but Valdis could make out that the man behind was carrying a pistol – and it was pointing straight at him.

'Who are you?'

'We're with the British government, Foreign Office. This chap here is my colleague, Tim Harper,' said the tall man, gesturing towards his companion with the gun. 'And I'm David Williams.' Neither were their real names. In reality Harper's name was Phillip Hardy and the tall man wearing a dark raincoat, thick spectacles and calling himself David Williams was Archie Anderson. They were both officers of Britain's Secret Intelligence Service, MI6.

While Philby had recognised his apprehension as dread, Valdis Ozols now felt in his gut the first tentative surge of excitement.

The three men walked around the side of the warehouse to where a big Jaguar saloon was parked. Hardy got into the driver's seat. Anderson ushered Valdis into the back and walked over to the other side, moving in alongside him. Valdis had never been in car a like this. As they drove silently towards the port's gates, he tried to settle himself into the comfort of the leather seats, but his thoughts were confused, tumbling over one another in a disordered torrent. He'd just been abducted at gunpoint. His ship was about to sail and here he was sitting beside this strange foreigner heading away from the security of the vessel, which to all intents and purposes was his home. And yet, this was it, surely. But dare he allow himself such a thought? He'd known the English spy Philby was coming aboard and that they would take him to the Black Sea port of Odessa from where he'd be transferred to Moscow. Now here he was in this beautiful car with these two strangers.

Anderson interrupted his thoughts: 'Relax, Comrade. You're in safe hands. Here, have a cigar.'

Valdis took one from the proffered leather pouch. Anderson lit it and then lit one for himself. He opened the window a fraction to let the smoke out into the darkness, but not far enough for the rain to get in. The car's interior was warm. The smell of leather and cigars enveloped them. They were heading north towards the outskirts of the city now as Anderson pulled down the walnut tray table set into the back of the driver's seat and gestured to Valdis to do the same before opening the central drinks cabinet set on the floor between them. He placed two crystal tumblers from the cabinet onto the tray tables then retrieved a steel flask and carefully poured large measures of whisky into each glass.

'Laphroaig – a malt from the Hebridean isle of Islay. An acquired taste but I like it. *Nostrovia!*'

'English,' said Valdis. 'I prefer to speak English.'

'Good. Cheers then!' That's a good sign, thought Anderson, also switching to English. 'Here's to friendship.'

As they clinked their glasses and the car sped north on the road to Byblos, the *Dolmatova* passed into the fairway, through the protective arms of the breakwater and out into the tempestuous Mediterranean. Philby sat on his bunk in a cabin that smelled of sweat. He was already well into a bottle of Ararat brandy. As the ship began to pitch and roll in the heavy swell, he felt the bile rising in his throat. He stood up, struggling to keep his balance, staggered over to the cracked washbasin in the corner of the cabin and threw up.

It was almost midnight on the 23rd of January 1963.

Chapter 2

Byblos, Lebanon

January/February 1963

The safe house they took Valdis to was set in the hills above the city of Byblos, not far from its twelfth-century castle and some twenty-five miles north of Beirut.

'One of the oldest cities in the world, you know,' Hardy, a resident of Beirut, had informed them as they approached, in what was to become a running commentary on the history of the Lebanon. 'First occupied ten thousand years ago they reckon. Early Neolithic.'

'Really,' Anderson had replied, his mind elsewhere. He was quietly satisfied with how smoothly the abduction had gone. Almost too well – but that was his suspicious mind, he told himself. Before he went to bed that first night he called his wife, Evelyn. She knew better than to ask what he was up to, though could tell from his tone that whatever it was had gone well. Instead she gave him an update on how the family was doing back in England. Their sixteen-year-old son, who was studying at Harrow, had some big exams approaching. And, of course, the weather was dreadful with the whole country snowbound and frozen up in the worst winter for years. They chatted on for ten minutes or so of mundane domestic matters before exchanging a few more intimate words and calling off, with Anderson promising to ring again in a few days.

Then, sitting in the living room looking out at the storm through the French windows of the villa and with Valdis safely under Hardy's watchful eye in an upstairs bedroom, he savoured a final nip of Laphroaig and pondered over the events of the last few days. He had, in the course of several meetings, obtained the signed confession from Philby, his old friend but now his nemesis, that he'd been sent to Beirut to secure. He'd given him two options: either be returned to London to face trial at the Old Bailey on charges of treason, followed almost certainly by a life sentence, or, if he confessed to everything including names of agents, moles and secrets he'd revealed to his masters in Moscow, defection. There had been a third option which Anderson had presented in the form of a hard, silent stare across the table. Both men knew what that was: expedient demise. But it didn't need spelling out.

Then, having secured Philby's confession, he had orchestrated an agreement with the KGB's head of station to transport Philby to Moscow by whatever means were available. Finally, knowing from his sources in Naval Intelligence that the *Dolmatova* was in port and that her young political officer was quite possibly ripe for plucking, he'd nabbed Valdis Ozols from under the noses of his masters. It had been too good an opportunity to miss. Political officers had other responsibilities besides ensuring their fellow shipmates conformed with Soviet doctrine, and it was these that interested him.

The question of how to handle the young Latvian had not been discussed at any great length in London. Anderson wanted to control the enrolment process, the debriefing and subsequent briefing himself. This wasn't because he was controlling by nature. On the contrary, he was generally compliant in his dealings with colleagues, including his superiors. But Valdis was different. Anderson felt bitterly let down by Philby's treachery; it was a deeply personal matter for him. Not only that, but he knew some of the stain that the whole scandalous business had left on the Service's reputation, particularly in the eyes of their sister service, MI5, however small, had tarnished him and others too for not having recognised signs of Philby's duplicity earlier. Rationally speaking that wasn't fair and C himself had been at pains to tell him and his colleagues not to dwell on it. Nevertheless, Anderson knew that the successful recruitment of such a potentially valuable, long-term asset as Valdis Ozols was a means by which he could restore what he believed to be his dented reputation – a redemption of sorts.

As often happened, his mind went back to the war. Seconded to Lisbon, his job had been to monitor anti-British activity in the city and in doing so he'd become a highly effective field officer, not least in securing the defection of two senior German intelligence officers, a coup that had severely damaged the effectiveness of Germany's foreign intelligence service, the Abwehr. He was proud of this achievement and looked back on those days with some nostalgia. He was proud too that the operation was still used as a case study in the Service's training programme. Now, as a senior MI6 officer, he still enjoyed a high degree of independence which he was determined to put to good use in his handling of Valdis Ozols.

He slept well that night but woke early to the sound of the wind thrashing the branches of the trees outside his bedroom window. And it was as he lay in bed reflecting on the events of the previous day that unbidden doubts began to creep into his mind. In his business no one could ever be completely trusted. He didn't need reminding of that. Lies, betrayal, subterfuge: these were all part and parcel of his trade. As a field agent during the war he had practised many of these black arts himself and was good at it. So now he wondered, was it wise to take his young recruit's loyalty for granted? For now perhaps, but it was always possible that as time went by, circumstances might cause Valdis Ozols to regret hasty decisions taken in his younger days. Or worse, it was possible, although he judged unlikely, that Ozols was a plant skilfully put in place by the Soviets to operate as a triple. Eager to deal with these disturbing thoughts, Anderson rose from his bed and stepped out onto the balcony. The storm was passing but the wind was still strong enough to bend the branches of the trees in the garden below as dark, ragged clouds raced across the early morning sky. He laughed to himself. Of course he was right to feel these concerns. Wasn't it his job to be suspicious? More than that, it had become second nature. But it did no harm to remind himself to take nothing for granted. Assumption, after all, was the mother of all cock-ups.

***

A bright, breezy February morning in the second week of the Byblos safe house sessions. A routine had been established: they would meet for breakfast at eight, prepared by either Hardy or Anderson himself. Anderson had toyed with the idea of employing the elderly couple who owned the villa to perform domestic chores but in the end decided against it. They'd been vetted by the Beirut station but on discussing it with Hardy they'd both decided not to risk having anyone else in the house, vetted or not. By nine-thirty they'd be seated at the dining room table and the questioning would begin. They hadn't mentioned the recording devices hidden around the house which had been installed before their arrival, and Valdis Ozols hadn't asked whether he was being monitored.

Anderson looked across the table at the Latvian. He was, he thought, physically at least, not unlike himself: not as tall, but dark-haired, skinny, with a pallid complexion and a high forehead – even the same round-framed glasses. At first he'd been jumpy and wary. But now he'd had time to get used to what was happening to him, he was relaxed and a quiet air of confidence had replaced the edginess.

Much of what Valdis divulged was already known to them, but not all. Anderson had made the initial overtures to the KGB Beirut station chief, proposing that it would be better for all concerned, including Philby himself, if he were settled in some obscure Moscow suburb rather than incarcerated in London's Wormwood Scrubs prison where the British media could keep the spotlight on him with speculation as to every detail of his life inside. Better to hide him away somewhere far from England. And after consultation with Moscow, this was what had been agreed. What Anderson hadn't known and Valdis now revealed, was that Philby's KGB masters had made it clear to him that if he refused the move to Moscow, he might well face a sticky end there in Beirut courtesy of a KGB hit squad. The last thing the Soviets wanted was Philby revealing everything he knew of KGB methods and operations to British Intelligence beyond that which he might already have told Anderson. Should that happen, or even look as if it might, then he would need to be silenced for good. All this Valdis had learned in the senior officers' mess on board the *Dolmatova*: loose talk in the days and nights while the ship had been working cargo in Beirut's port and awaiting their British passenger.

These revelations had astounded Anderson. Learning that Valdis had had the ear of senior intelligence officers on board the *Dolmatova* presented the opportunity of questioning the young Latvian further as to the reality of life on a Soviet merchant vessel engaged in covert intelligence operations: a spy ship. And Valdis had been only too happy to tell of his own role as a political officer on the ships of Morflot, the overarching, state-controlled fleet management entity which, besides controlling well over half of the country's imports and exports, played a vital support role to Soviet naval operations. This was a subject of particular interest to Anderson. There were over a thousand vessels under the Soviet flag including those of satellite states such as Latvia. The ships' political officers were not directly employed by either the GRU – the Soviet military intelligence organisation – or by the KGB. They were employees of Morflot. But it was generally accepted by Britain's own Naval Intelligence and by the Americans too, that the GRU had access to Morflot's reports and enjoyed considerable influence over its activities. Not only this, but it also gave clues as to the working relationship between the KGB and the GRU, often judged to be a hostile one.

Ostensibly the political officer's role was to stimulate and maintain party morale and discipline on board, and to detect and report any signs of dissent. In such matters their authority exceeded that of the ship's captain. The crews were normally granted shore leave, even in such centres of capitalist decadence as Hong Kong, Hamburg or New York, hence the need for some faithful party comrade to keep an eye on their activities. Furthermore, the political officers were expected to serve as the GRU's eyes and ears in the ports where the ships called. How many more of Valdis Ozols' persuasion were there? Disillusioned young men sailing the high seas and under orders to nose around the world's commercial ports on behalf of their masters back in Moscow? Imagine, mused Anderson, if we could identify and recruit such officers. It would be a long-term project of course, but one worth pursuing, not only in terms of the intelligence harvest it would reap, but for the effect it would have of undermining the state's authority. When he'd put it to Valdis he'd been highly receptive to the idea too; anything to destabilise the apparatus of the Soviet state towards which he harboured such contempt.

But while all this was useful, Anderson had to proceed with caution. British Naval Intelligence had tipped off their counterparts in MI6 that the young political officer of the *Dolmatova* had form, and this was well worth exploring further. The previous year, the *Dolmatova* had been one of a fleet of ships engaged in Operation Anadyr and, as Peter Hardy brought in a fresh jug of coffee, it was this part of the story that Anderson now wanted to broach.

Chapter 3

Byblos, Lebanon

February 1963

Operation Anadyr: what didn't they know, these British? Their sources must be good, very good, Valdis told himself. It had all happened just the previous year. And he remembered every detail as if it were yesterday.

The *Dolmatova*, his ship then, as it had been up until a fortnight ago, had laid alongside in the Latvian port of Liepaya for several weeks preparing for the voyage. Neither her crew nor the troops, who were embarking by the dozen, had had any clear idea what their destination was, never mind the real purpose of the voyage. The whole port was locked down from the outside world with guards posted at all gates to prevent unauthorised personnel leaving or entering. 'A strategic exercise in the far north of the USSR' was all they were told. Rumours were they'd be heading for the island of Novaya Zemlya. Among the equipment being loaded were skis, boots and fleece-lined parkas. And then there were the SS-4 missiles and their launchers stowed in the holds with tractors, harvesters and other agricultural equipment lashed down on the deck above for reasons which could only be guessed at. Combine harvesters to the Arctic? Eventually they'd sailed from the Baltic and out into the North Sea.

From there they headed around the north coast of Scotland and into the Atlantic, which was when Valdis was called up to the captain's cabin where, along with other senior officers, he was told a little of what was going on.

'We are on course for the Caribbean,' announced the skipper. 'Cuba to deliver the troops and the missiles too. Do not ask questions. I will either not know or not be permitted to give you the answers.' And that had been that.

Officially, interaction between the ship's crew and the troops was not allowed, but conditions where the troops were housed became almost unbearable as they approached the tropics and the temperature below decks approached 50 degrees centigrade during the day. So the crew would do what they could to alleviate the soldiers' torment by hosing them down from above and permitting them out on deck for short periods outside the approved times. But as they grew closer to their destination, these concessions were terminated to hide them from the prying eyes of the US Air Force flying overhead. Eventually, after eighteen days at sea, they'd reached the port of Mariel, thirty miles west of Havana. And it was here that Valdis had run into trouble.

How, Valdis asked himself now, could the British have learned what had happened? They must have good agents in Cuba. Or was it the Americans? Or most likely, dissident Cuban groups? Whoever it was, the story had got back to

Anderson and here he was in Lebanon being interrogated about it.

As with most cases of seafarers getting into trouble in port, it was a combination of alcohol and sex. Normally it was Valdis who would be responsible for sorting out such matters, but this time he himself had become the problem. A quiet bar away from the port, one too many Saoco cocktails and the most beautiful girl he had ever seen in his life. It was love, or infatuation, or both, inducing a kind of madness that took hold at first sight, and for the first time in his life. They'd spent the night together in a little room which faced onto a dirt track beyond which was the ocean. As he recounted it to the two British agents, every detail came flooding back to him – vividly, painfully. Delfina had not been a bar girl, she was a student. She'd been in the bar with friends. They'd got talking and one thing had led to another. She had told him of her family. Her father was a lawyer and her mother a teacher. Before the revolution they had been members of the prosperous middle classes, but that had all changed after 1959 and her parents deeply resented how their livelihoods had been affected by the Communist regime. Delfina though had been more accepting of the situation and had decided to follow her mother's profession. She was studying to be a teacher.

'Valdis! You alright old chap?' It was Anderson, interrupting his thoughts.

'Yes, I am alright,' he replied irritably. 'What is it you want to know? How many times we made love?'

'No, no, no, of course not. Just relax. Let's take a break shall we?'

'What? To go out do you mean? Is that safe?'

'Don't worry. We have our own people watching. We are alerted to anything suspicious.'

Valdis didn't seem reassured. Anderson's almost casual attitude was beginning to make him nervous. He had yet to learn that it was a carefully cultivated and typically British veneer. But the excursion had an ulterior motive. Both MI6 men would be keeping their eyes skinned for any sign they were being followed. They left the safe house and walked through winding streets lined with restaurants and bars just beginning to open for the lunchtime trade. Their destination was the Citadel, a twelfth-century Crusader castle still largely intact and the source of many historical facts and legends set in what was claimed to be the world's oldest city. Here Hardy was in his element, acting as tour guide as they climbed amid the ruins and ramparts. They used the area not just to watch for followers, their own people as well as KGB, but to give Valdis a sense for what was to come. They moved on into the Temple of Baalat Gebal, and to a row of royal tombs cut in vertical shafts deep into the rock, dating back to the second millennium BC and including that of King Ahiram which bore the sinister inscription: 'Warning here. Thy death is below.' Ominous, thought Anderson and they returned to the house. Hardy had spotted one of his colleagues from the Beirut office but there had been no sign of the KGB – not that they'd detected.

Hardy began preparing lunch. The old couple who owned the place, Bachir and Elissa, were Maronite Christians. Hardy knew them well and had used their home as a safe house on previous occasions. Now they called to deliver groceries and wine, greeting him sociably and asking if all was well. They chatted and Hardy placed an order for a few items he needed. Hardy liked to cook. It left Anderson and Valdis to talk outside in the garden together. Such a device could break down defences put up by the presence of two interrogators questioning one subject. But since working and cohabiting with Anderson he'd had another reason to want to cook: Anderson was no good at it. In fact, he was barely a cook at all, claiming his signature dish as poached eggs and beans on toast, and even this would often result in burnt toast and the eggs set solid. When Hardy's chicken *fatteh* was ready, he called them in. Anderson poured wine and they ate.

But Valdis remained withdrawn. They'd intruded into an intimate corner of his heart, of his secret memories, and he resented it. The truth was he still desperately missed his Cuban girl. What he didn't tell them was not only did he still love Delfina, but that she had been his first lover. The consequences of their illicit night together had almost been disastrous. He'd returned to the ship the following afternoon. His position was such that the captain could not challenge him directly about his absence and Valdis had cooked up a story about shadowing a group of young crewmembers who he'd seen talking to local men in the bar, before leaving with them. He'd thought the encounter was suspicious so had kept a watch on them all night. They'd been playing poker and drinking heavily. In the end they'd gone off with a group of girls the local men had found for them. Valdis had decided it was his duty to protect them should they fall into harm's way. But political officers were often the least popular sailors on the ship and his story was not corroborated by the sailors themselves. It was his word against theirs, but the captain didn't believe Valdis's story either and reported him to the Morflot officer already stationed in Mariel. On his return to Latvia he'd been signed off the ship and was promptly ordered to report to Morflot's head office in Moscow, where a team of GRU officers subjected him to a three-day grilling. Valdis had broken on the second day and told them what had really happened. They'd tried to establish the identity of the girl but Valdis had kept that to himself. In the end he'd got away with a severe reprimand and a month's pay docked. If it had happened anywhere else the matter might have been dealt with more leniently, but this wasn't anywhere else. It was Cuba.

Valdis worried now that distrust might have formed in the minds of his British interrogators. So he pulled out a dog-eared black and white photograph from his wallet and passed it across the table. Anderson looked at it, then at Valdis. 'She's beautiful,' Anderson muttered quietly. 'I do apologise if you thought we were doubting you.'

Valdis barely heard him. His mind had drifted back to Cuba: the warmth and sunshine, the luxuriant tropical greenery, the light-hearted, fun-loving people, and that night with Delfina. One day, he thought.

But the seeds of something else had been sown in Cuba; something which for Anderson was far more interesting than a fling with a pretty local girl. As he had watched the crated missiles being unloaded and trucked away from the port for further assembly, for the first time Valdis had begun to think of the consequences of what he was a part of. Now, at this dining-room table many months later, he spoke, his voice harsh with the strength of his feelings.

'That night, after we had made love, I told Delfina of my fears. Of missiles we had brought to her country. I had seen the cargo we were carrying and I knew what it could do to her and her family, and to humanity. We had no right to be doing this. I was angry and I told her then what I had to do with my life. And that is why I knew that sooner or later I would need to be talking to someone like you, having these conversations.'

All this was a huge relief to Anderson. The report he'd received from London was quite different from the account Valdis was now giving. According to the report, his absence from the ship in Cuba had never been explained and it was thought he might have been engaged in some covert operation that would need to be clarified. Instead, it seemed, it had been a tryst between two lovers that had led the young seafarer to make a decision that would alter the course of his life. It was a credible explanation that added to the picture he was building up of the man. Anderson had spent half his life trying to make sense of people's actions and motivations, and build judgements based on that. He was as certain as he could be now that Valdis was telling the truth about the lost night in Cuba. And he was equally convinced of the man's determination to betray the system that he so detested.

The debriefing was completed late the following day. Now Anderson would turn to what was just as important, if not more so: the briefing and the construction of a plausible legend placing Valdis in a position whereby he could safely gather and convey useful intelligence back to London, while avoiding the suspicions of his masters. The operation would start with delivering Valdis into the arms of the GRU. There was no sense in pretending that he had simply missed the ship's sailing from Beirut and gone AWOL in Lebanon for two weeks. Neither the KGB nor the GRU would swallow that. If the deception were to work, there had to be at least some truth to it. Yes, he'd been abducted, but no, he had not been turned.

The answer was not long in presenting itself: a spy swap. There was never a shortage of candidates for this kind of trade, but London had already been working on a particular exchange that would see the British Council teacher, Karl Thompson, returned safely to his home in England. Thompson had been arrested in Warsaw two years previously and convicted on various espionage charges, including inciting his Polish students to foment unrest among the population. He'd been tried in Moscow, sentenced to twelve years and incarcerated first in Lubyanka before being transferred to a lunatic asylum somewhere east of the Urals where he had reportedly suffered beatings and other forms of mistreatment. His health had deteriorated to the point that the British government was under rising pressure from his family, and from Amnesty International and other human rights organisations, to secure his release.

Now in return, the Soviets would get Valdis Ozols back. Anderson liked the idea, not least because it would tighten Valdis's legend of the unwilling victim of a kidnapping by MI6. It was just a matter of arranging the exchange, a sensitive task at any time. But what worried him more was the treatment Valdis would have to suffer once in the pitiless hands of the GRU, who lacked the subtlety and finesse of their more sophisticated cousins in the KGB and who would want to test his cover to breaking point. The GRU being a part of the Soviet military apparatus had bred this culture, Anderson knew, and now, in addition, he began to worry that the GRU's reputation for clumsiness would increase the risk of the exchange going awry.

'No, don't worry,' Valdis had assured him. 'I know the GRU. I know how they think. Better them than those clever KGB bastards.'

The stratagem was simple. The Soviets had to retrieve Valdis and believe without doubt that he had not been turned; that he had remained loyal to the Soviet state throughout his incarceration and had resisted all the Brits' efforts to seduce him into a life of treachery. They both knew that however convincingly he proclaimed this falsehood, he would still have to endure days, if not weeks, of penetrating interrogation. He would have to rely on the trail of deception laid down by Anderson and his people, and on his own dogged resolve to deny all the accusations that might be levelled against him.

That evening, Anderson opened a bottle of wine, which they drank between them before dinner.

'Did you know,' enthused Hardy as he poured the wine, 'that Lebanon is one of the oldest sites of wine production in the world? The Israelite prophet Hosea urged his followers to return to God so that "they will blossom as the vine, and their fragrance will be like the wine of Lebanon". That was almost three thousand years ago!' They opened another bottle to drink with their dinner, but Valdis declined. He *had* been turned – readily. Now he had to live with the consequences of his decision.

Chapter 4

Al-Husn, Syria

February 1963

Krak des Chevaliers was a seventy-mile drive from Byblos. They entered Syria via the Abboudieh–Dabboussieh border, crossing well before noon. They had visas arranged by the Beirut station and Anderson had a few fifty and hundred dollar bills in his pocket in case of any hesitation on the part of the border police.

Hardy had argued that as an experienced field agent it was he who should handle the potentially dangerous switch, but Anderson had insisted he must be the one despite the risks.

'That's exactly my point,' he'd stressed. 'They'll see you for who you are – a tough, hardened field agent.' Hardy was six foot four and weighed two hundred pounds plus. 'You're probably on their files, as might I be. But I'm the ageing, desk-bound boffin in their eyes – the least dangerous. And I need to see this go right, Phillip. There's a great deal riding on it. I'm talking about the future, the long game. He's my Joe now. And I'll make sure he's the best asset we've ever had over there.' The truth was that Anderson had formed a genuine affection for Valdis, viewing him almost as a surrogate son: unprofessional, but true nonetheless.

Anderson was driving a Simca with Valdis alongside him. They kept a close eye on the heavy traffic around them but the nondescript car their Beirut people had acquired was unlikely to attract attention. As an added precaution, Hardy was driving the shiny Jaguar some miles behind and would veer off somewhere enroute to create a diversion, though only if he deemed it necessary. Otherwise he'd tail them all the way. Their fear was that a KGB team from Beirut might have their own agenda, or simply not be aware of what their GRU cousins were up to. It was not unheard-of for one of the Russian intelligence services to trip over the other during an operation.

'I hope to hell this is going to work, Archie,' Hardy had said as he saw them off.

'Relax, will you. You'll be there as back-up.' He might have been the desk-bound boffin nowadays but he'd done his time in the field, and in times of war when the stakes and the danger were at their highest.

Hardy knew Anderson pretty well and knew his blasé style, which was something of a hallmark back in London, but he was feeling the tension and wasn't too comfortable at being relegated to back-up rather than running the show. Anderson was in his late forties. He was short-sighted and not particularly athletic, while Hardy was at least ten years younger, skied, played tennis and swam – often all on the same day. He prided himself on his fitness. And he'd been based in Lebanon for almost three years now, during which time he'd had one or two brushes with local Soviet agents. Both men were armed but Hardy went to a discreet firing range outside the city once a week for target practice with his Browning. He had no idea when Anderson had last fired a gun.

And most important of all was Valdis. He looked calm enough, but how would he cope if this charade turned awkward?

Anderson parked the Simca in the village of al-Husn, which nestled at the foot of the ancient fortress over two thousand feet up from the coast. A local man approached them offering to keep an eye on the car. Anderson handed him fifty dollars with the promise of another fifty, provided all was well on their return.

Declining the enthusiastic offers of the local guides, they climbed up through the main entrance gate set into the castle's sixteen foot thick walls, across the moat and into a courtyard. Valdis paused, placing his hand on Anderson's sleeve.

'I'm sorry,' he said, his voice suddenly wavering. 'Give me a moment, please.' He was clearly agitated. He glanced about him uncertainly, rubbing the back of his neck.

'Deep breath,' Anderson said. 'It'll be alright, trust me.' He took hold of the Latvian's arms and stared him in the eye. Suddenly he recalled a similar situation when seeing his son off to boarding school on his first day. Only this wasn't Harrow. And there'd be no half-term or summer holidays to look forward to.

'I have something important to give you,' he said. He'd saved this until the last moment because he'd anticipated the fear that Valdis would be feeling and wanted to give him both reassurance and something to concentrate on, something to take his mind off what lay ahead. 'You must memorise this, do you understand?' He took a notebook from his pocket and held it up. 'It's the number you can call in an emergency. It's untraceable and it will take you straight through to me at any time, day or night, wherever I am.' He recited the number and told Valdis to repeat it three times. 'Got it?'

'Got it,' said Valdis, feeling better.

They entered a dark passageway covered in delicate carvings which led through to a large vaulted hall. This eight hundred-year-old castle, built for the Knights of St John at the height of their powers, had housed a garrison of two thousand men. Now it was to be the stage for a poorly rehearsed play. Anderson had handled spy swaps before, but never one like this. He was casting his young protégé into a life of uncertainty and danger. The weight of responsibility hung heavy on the spy master's shoulders. If he'd got this wrong … It didn't bear thinking about.

Chapter 5

Damascus–al-Husn, Syria

February 1963

On rising at seven that same morning, Lieutenant Colonel Vladimir Rybakov of the GRU's Spetsnaz 10th Special Purpose Brigade, had smiled, not something he allowed himself very often. But this morning he was feeling good. He lit the first cigarette of the sixty or so he would smoke that day, coughed as he inhaled and stood naked, looking out of his bedroom window. The sun was shining and today he had a small task to perform, not something he would normally be assigned, it was more KGB territory, but this was different. He was in the right place at the right time, having just completed a tour of duty in the Chechnya, Ingushetia and Dagestan borderlands. Now he'd been redeployed to Syria, another godforsaken outpost of the Soviet empire. There were compensations though: a day trip from Damascus to the famous Crusader castle of Krak des Chevaliers didn't seem too arduous.

The Englishman, Karl Thompson, had arrived the day before on a direct VVS flight from Moscow. They'd delivered him to Rybakov's unit on the outskirts of the city, where he was locked in a cell normally reserved for Soviet soldiers who'd got themselves into trouble with the

Komendantskaya sluzhba, the Soviet military police. Rybakov had visited him and found a man broken by his experiences. When he'd entered Thompson's cell the Englishman had looked up from his bunk with fear in his eyes as if waiting for a beating from the burly Russian, something he'd come to expect from the living hell he'd been going through. His nerves were in tatters, his state of mind surging from almost hysterical optimism to the depths of depression as the months had gone by. The beatings he'd almost learned to live with, but the psychological damage was another matter. His sanity was on the edge, his grip on reality loosened amid the constantly shifting, raised and dashed hopes of his incarceration.

'Well, English. So you're going home, eh?' Rybakov had bellowed, taunting the man. 'Let's hope so, eh? Let's hope the other guy turns up, eh? Otherwise you may get stuck here – in the desert, with me!' Roaring with laughter he'd left the cell and walked back down the corridor.

Today, he was taking Thompson and two of his most trusted men with him. The roads were poor so they would leave at nine o'clock sharp, safely allowing four hours for the hundred and thirty mile journey. Once there they would make the swap with the British and head back north to Damascus, arriving before dark. He was not anticipating trouble but if there was any it would add a touch of excitement to the day. Trouble was something Rybakov was used to, even sought out. The young Latvian seaman he'd been told to pick up in exchange for Thompson was none of his concern. He'd leave it to the GRU interrogation people in Moscow to hammer the truth out of him, although he wouldn't mind a crack at him first. As for the British who were delivering him, Rybakov had never rated them much and his judgement had been supported by their handling of Philby. It amazed him that they hadn't just shot the bastard. A traitor was a traitor whoever's side you were on.

He finished his cigarette, threw the stub out of the window, turned back to the bed where the young Syrian woman lay sleeping, pulled the sheet back and slapped her backside. 'Wake up, little one!' he boomed. 'Time for some fun before I go to work, eh!' She was a pretty little thing, far more accommodating than those Muslim women in the Caucasus. They'd resisted the attentions of Rybakov and the men of his unit. Some would call it rape. He didn't care. Soldiers needed entertainment and some relief wherever they were fighting. As for the summary executions and the torture, he didn't particularly relish carrying out such acts, but they were necessary if order was to be restored among those people who thought they had some God-given right to govern themselves. At the end of the day he didn't care about them or their religion. He was just glad to be out of the place, even if it was to another shithole. The north Caucasus might be quiet for now but he'd seen enough during his tours in the region to know there would be trouble in the future. And the same went for Syria.

***

The Russians, along with Thompson, arrived a quarter of an hour before the Brits with Valdis, but instead of entering the hall as had been agreed, they positioned themselves in one of the cloistered passageways off to one side and from where they could observe the comings and goings. Rybakov had no trouble spotting the three men when they arrived.

'Welcome, Mr MI6!' he called out, his deep bass echoing through the hall. Startled tourists looked round to see where the voice was coming from. 'Come here! We have your man. And you have mine, I can see.'

Anderson took Valdis by the arm and led him into an adjacent passageway. Hardy had joined them and stood a few yards behind. It took them several moments to adjust to the darkness. Then they saw the Russians. Anderson called out: 'I have Ozols here. Now show me Thompson.'

Four figures at the far end of the passageway moved forward into a narrow patch of sunlight cast from an arrow slit in the wall. Now Anderson could make them out, one, a thickset bull of a man, holding another by the arm: Thompson. And two others behind, flanking them.

Rybakov called out again: 'Here he is. Now send me Ozols.'

Anderson could see now that Rybakov was holding a gun to Thompson's head. 'They pass each other in the middle, alright?' he called. 'That's the protocol. And put that gun away.'

But as he spoke Thompson suddenly broke free of the Russian's grasp lurching forward in an awkward run, heading straight for where Anderson and Valdis were standing. Anderson could hear his rasping breath as, panicked, he made a desperate rush away from what he must have perceived to be the threat of Rybakov and his gun, to safety.

'Stop there!' Anderson shouted, in that instant fearing the Russians' response . A shot rang out, echoing round the castle walls and Thompson was thrown forward. Collapsing onto the stone floor, he convulsed once or twice then lay still. After a moment of stunned silence, screams rang out from the tourists in the hall.

'Go now, run!' Anderson whispered to Valdis. The Latvian got the message and as he burst forward, started shouting in Russian: *'Pomogi mne!'* Feinting, Anderson made to grab him by the arm. Improvising the charade, Valdis struggled, broke free and shouting again, *'Pomogi!'* Help! ran towards the Russians.

Anderson rushed over to where Thompson lay, feeling his neck for a pulse. There was none. He stood up, stepping back to avoid the pool of blood spreading out from the body. 'You mad bastard!' he shouted at Rybakov, 'what the hell did you do that for?'

'Hey, English,' called Rybakov. 'Easy, alright? Easy! He shouldn't have run like that, the fool. I told him I'd shoot him if he tried anything stupid, so what did he do? Something stupid!'

A few tourists had entered the passageway now to gawp at the unfolding drama. The other two Russians had drawn their guns as Anderson moved away from the dead man and towards them. Hardy had his Browning drawn and was walking beside Anderson.

Rybakov spoke softly now: 'Let's not turn this into a big problem, eh? Your man was sick; he was dying. He wouldn't have lasted long, believe me.'

'You broke the deal,' Anderson replied bitterly. 'This won't go down well for you in Moscow.'

'I think you mean in London, my friend. This one belongs to us. You see?' Rybakov had Valdis by the arm now and was shaking him gently. 'He wants to come back home, don't you, Ozols? He's a law-abiding citizen of the Soviet Union and you abducted him. Now, English,' the Russian added soothingly, 'all okay, yes? You go back to your office now. Tell your boss you fucked up again, eh? First you let Philby go, now this one.' He waved the gun towards where Thompson lay. 'Maybe time to retire,' he sneered. 'You're getting too old for this kind of work.'

'Take the little shit.' Anderson spoke angrily. 'He's no bloody use to us.'

***

Reflecting on it with Hardy back at the safe house that evening the two men agreed it had almost gone to plan. Their main objective had been achieved: they'd delivered Valdis to the Soviets with as strong a legend as they could for his protection. In time, when and only when Valdis made contact through the protocols Anderson had taught him, London could expect to harvest the fruits of his labour. But Anderson felt little satisfaction now the job was done. Only anxiety for his young Joe, and for the grilling he would soon have to endure. For his own noble and ideological reasons Valdis would be risking everything: exposure, interrogation, torture and a bullet in the back of his head.

As for Karl Thompson, there were always casualties in war, not least in the Cold War, but his was a particularly tragic case. Rybakov was a thug, a typical product of the GRU's Spetsnaz special forces. His masters would not approve of his impulsive behaviour in killing the Englishman. By casually shooting the man, he'd breached the terms of the deal brokered at a high level between Moscow and London. In doing so he'd damaged what little trust existed in Anglo–Soviet relations. Not irreparably, perhaps, but it would certainly make future deals of this nature all the more difficult.

'The KGB would have handled it better,' said Hardy over his whisky glass.

'Probably,' Anderson replied.

'Either way,' said Hardy, 'Thompson was another victim of the Soviet state. We know what we're up against, don't we.'

'Yes,' Anderson concluded, raising his glass. 'One of the most brutal, ruthless, unprincipled, oppressive and authoritarian states the world has ever seen, which is why we get up and go to work every day, eh? Here's to Valdis.'

PART 2

Chapter 6

Suez Canal, Egypt–Riga, Latvia

March 1999

We'd arrived at the southern end of the Suez Canal at 1700. Instructions from port control were to heave up anchor and have engines on standby for 0400 the following day, ready for the pilot to board. The next morning, bad weather meant a delay and we were told the pilot would now board at a different marker further north. We entered the canal itself at 0615, taking our position in the northbound convoy with four ships ahead of us.

'Angus, have your deck crew standing by on VHF to pick up the pilot, *endaxi*?'

'Standing by,' I called back to the chief mate.

The current was setting north-east at a rate of three knots and the *Haboub* wind was howling in from the north west at Beaufort six. The wind brought dust and sand with it, creating a thick haze that darkened the sky. The canal is a hundred miles long, give or take a mile or two. Because there are no locks to interrupt traffic, transit time from end to end averages fourteen or fifteen hours. Our old tub pushed on as best she could, although this time it took longer thanks to the adverse winds.

The *Electra M* had a take-it-or-leave-it look about her. She was built twenty-one years ago in Korea, not so old in ship years, but she'd been worked hard throughout her life and now the main engine was running on reduced revs due to an assortment of mechanical problems.

Once through the canal we had four days in Port Said taking on bunkers, stores and spares, making a few crew changes and waiting for the Greek repair squad who'd come down from Piraeus to finish repairs on the main engine.

My department had its fair share of problems too. Despite our best efforts *Rattus Rattus* continued to make his presence felt throughout the ship and the additional traps we needed to keep the rodents at bay hadn't arrived despite having been ordered weeks before; neither were they available from the Port Said chandler.

'Let's get a cat,' I'd suggested to the captain on many occasions. This had been the time-honoured solution for centuries.

'One of these days, Angus,' he'd reply.

Lifeboat stores overdue for replenishment was another problem. We hadn't received permission to purchase them from head office. Then two of my deck crew feared they'd picked up a dose of the clap while sampling the delights of Port Said's brothels. I sent them to the second mate for treatment in his capacity as the ship's medic.

On the positive side, replacement parts for the fresh water pumps had arrived, which meant we could all get proper showers. And the locals I dealt with were generally friendly and helpful – once I'd handed out the baksheesh: cartons of Marlboro and the odd bottle of Scotch from our bonded store. This was a task usually assigned to the skipper or the first mate, but I'd got landed with it. Pilots, agents, bumboat coxswains, mooring gangs: they all expected such gratuities, and once given would often ask for more. On this occasion it was the agent: 'For my brother, he is sick.'

'If he is sick he should stay away from the fags and the booze,' I said. 'He'll soon feel better.'

And although Joseph Conrad had called the canal a 'dismal but profitable ditch', which was true, Port Said itself, with its old turn of the century houses and their impressive wooden balconies several storeys high, the chaotic street markets and their noisy, cheerful vendors, all gave the city a kind of shabby charm – if you didn't have to live there.

We'd been moored to a buoy in one of the basins adjacent to the main channel. The wind was still blowing hard from the north-west. The waters were choppy and I watched as two of the mooring gang crouched on the buoy preparing to unshackle us, their little boat bobbing up and down in the swell a few yards away. I'd seen a similar situation in Hong Kong a year or so before when the Marine Department had ordered us to leave the harbour as a typhoon approached. Now the same thing was happening. The ship's weight was taken up by the chain cable and was pulling the whole assembly taut so they couldn't get the shackle pin out. It was stuck fast. In the absence of any deck officers, I called the bridge and they ordered the engineroom to give the engine a brief kick to dead slow and slacken off the chain. It solved the problem and we were on our way.

All this was on top of a long and frustrating voyage. Loading had been held up in Vietnam waiting for heavy monsoon rains to abate. Then halfway across the Indian Ocean the crankcase luboil pump had failed – a potentially catastrophic event if the crankshaft itself had become starved of oil. Crankcase explosions from this cause were not uncommon but fortunately our engineroom crew had acted in time to avoid a disaster. But it had meant three days drifting while they carried out temporary repairs, then a further delay installing a new pump in Port Said. Coupled with the heat, these events had caused stress and frayed tempers on what was normally a happy ship. The *Electra M*'s senior officers were Greek – old hands who'd been with the company for years. The junior officers were a mix of Croats and Poles with a couple of young Greek cadets. My ratings were a motley bunch of Filipinos, Tamils and Goanese. Motley, but one of the hardest-working crews I'd worked with.

Eventually we cleared Port Said, heading out into the Mediterranean shortly before 0700, some three weeks after departing from our load port in Vietnam. After the sweltering sand-laden heat of the Red Sea and the Suez Canal, it was a relief to feel the cool westerly breeze off our port bow. We'd loaded rice at Hai Phong, a trial shipment bound for the Baltic port of Riga. Fourteen days steaming, including a transit through the Straits of Gibraltar with its strong currents and high-density traffic, then out into the Atlantic swell where the ship began to dip and heave and the spring storms beckoned from Biscay; all this to look forward to before the heavy grey skies of the Baltic. It became much cooler now, with the crew donning sweaters and foul-weather jackets when working on deck. Seabirds circled, following us north on their summer migrations. Why not just stay south for the warmth, I wondered.

This would be my fourteenth month on the *Electra M*, meaning my leave was now overdue by five months. But I'd been sailing with Mavritis Maritime for three years and got on well with the owner, Christos Mavritis. He would come on board, often without prior notice and in unlikely places as we tramped our way from port to port finding whatever cargoes were available at attractive enough rates, a business at which Mavritis, like most Greek owners, was skilled.

I'd been bumped up from Able Seaman to Bosun, a kind of non-commissioned officer, after three months on my ship previous Mavritis ship, a promotion which meant more money but, as I was soon to find out, a whole lot of trouble too. One of these days, I told myself, I'd swallow the anchor and settle ashore. Plan A was to find work in Piraeus.

Apart from an Atlantic storm off the Portuguese coast it was an uneventful passage and, having welcomed the pilot on board, we eased through Riga's breakwater and, with a little help from a harbour tug and the river's current, came round neatly alongside the grain terminal, finished with engines at 0430 on a cold March morning.

The chief mate, an elderly Greek who'd been passed over for promotion to Master more times than anyone could remember, was worried how the cargo had fared with such extreme changes in temperature and humidity on the voyage north. So was I, and at first light, since the mate was no longer agile enough, I took a couple of ABs into each hold to carry out a thorough inspection, checking for signs of condensation. The Latvian government surveyor would be coming on board before discharge commenced and I didn't want any unpleasant surprises, such as having to condemn half the cargo due to wet damage. In the event there was damage to a dozen or so bags, but we'd not expected to get away without some wetting. So with surveyors and the chief mate all happy, discharge commenced using shore cranes. It was a slow process due to delays in the trucks arriving alongside and after a week our laytime had expired and we came onto demurrage, payable as compensation by the charterer to the owner on failure to discharge the cargo within the time agreed.

At length the holds were empty and we'd received instructions from our owners to proceed to an anchorage off Antwerp for further orders. That was at 1800 hours, the time when things began to go badly wrong – for me if not for anyone else.

'Captain wants to see you, Bosun,' called the chief mate. I walked back along the deck from the bosun's store beneath the forecastle where I'd been returning some tools and tackle we'd used during the cargo discharge, knocked on the door of the captain's day room and went in.

'Sit yourself down, Angus.' Captain Andreas Kynigos addressed me by my first name in a gesture of familiarity he didn't use for everyone. Communication with the officers was more formal to protect the necessary hierarchy that went with shipboard protocol. Also, it was Kynigos who'd recommended my promotion from AB to Bosun on our last ship. I didn't take his familiarity for granted. He was still the skipper. Ships' captains live an isolated life between sea and sky and for the most part are removed from everyday trivialities. It is this that helps command the respect of both their shipmates and those ashore.

'Young Petros, the cadet, hasn't returned from shore leave and we're due to sail in an hour. I want you to find him and bring him back – *fidee, fidee*!' Kynigos was as Greek as Aristotle but, like me, had sailed with Chinese crews and occasionally we'd exchange simple Cantonese phrases we'd picked up over the years.

'When did he go ashore?'

'Last night, 1900 I understand.'

'On his own?'

'Apparently. My best guess is there's a woman involved. Chief mate says he's been behaving love-struck for the last week or two. I've talked with some of the other officers who've seen him in the Blue Lady Bar in the Old Town. Best you go alone. If a whole gang of sailors turn up it might start trouble. You're okay with that aren't you?'

'Sure,' I said without feeling at all sure. The cadet was a young Greek signed on a few months back and to date had not struck me as being of much use.

'You know who he is?' I nodded. The missing cadet was also Christos Mavritis' nephew.

I'd been in the Blue Lady Bar myself a few days before with some shipmates. It was a hangout for hookers, pimps and a clientele comprising mostly dock workers and sailors of many nationalities. It smelled of beer and cheap perfume. I ordered an Aldaris beer and looked around as my eyes adjusted to the dim lighting. It didn't take me long to spot young Mavritis and his girl. They were seated in a cosy little alcove towards the back. I walked over slowly and sat down beside them with my beer, nice and friendly.

'Hi,' I said, addressing the girl. 'I'm Angus.' She looked at me. I was intruding on their space and it showed in her expression. She was wearing a blue sequined dress which barely hid her ample charms. And she was pretty. I could see why Petros had chosen her.

'I'm afraid our ship's due to sail, so Petros and I have to get back onboard now.'

'I'm staying here, man,' he announced. 'Not goin' anywhere.' His voice was slurred. He drew closer to the girl, putting his arm round her shoulder.

I didn't waste time trying to reason with him. I just reminded him that the captain as well as his uncle and his father would expect him to do his duty. He was a cadet officer and should set an example to his shipmates too. And failure to report back from shore leave was a serious offence. But I wasn't getting through to him.

'Tell him, will you?' I said to the girl. She just laughed so I got up, went round to his side of the table and put my hand on his shoulder.

'Have you paid for the drinks?'

'No, he hasn't,' said the girl.

'Okay, this should cover it,' I said and placed a fifty-dollar note on the table. She grabbed it and I pulled Petros up by his collar. He didn't offer much resistance and I managed to drag him out onto the street without too much of a disturbance in the bar.

It didn't last. We'd got less than a hundred yards down the road when a man came up from behind us, out of the shadows, quick and silent. I had my arm round Petros's shoulder. The man moved round, positioning himself in our path, a knife in his hand flashing with silver light. I stopped and stepped between Petros and the new arrival.

'Hi, what's the problem?' I was watching him closely, his body language and the knife.

'He's not paid for my girl. He's been with her and he's not paid.'

'Is that right, Petros?' But Petros was out of it. He mumbled something so I stepped back and shook him. He came to, a bit. 'I paid her already,' he shouted belligerently.

'How much does he owe you?' I asked, trying to calm things down. 'I gave her fifty bucks just now and Petros here says he's paid her too.'

'She's my girl. A grand. US!' he shouted. He was a tall, skinny guy, hopped-up, edgy, not behaving like he wanted to talk the matter through.

'We don't have that kind of money,' I said. 'Petro, how much have you got on you?'

Petros muttered something.

'What?' I shouted.

'Nothing! I got nothing left!'

I pulled out my remaining fifty-dollar note and handed it to the pimp. 'Here, take this. It's all I've got.'

'Fuck off! I said a grand. What else you got? Show me your watch.' He gave me an intense, fevered stare.

'Get lost will you?' I said, feeling the anger rising. 'Take the fifty and fuck off yourself.'

I'd wound him up more than I'd intended. It was a direct confrontation now, and I realised he was high as a kite, on cocaine I suspected. He'd taken a stance, leaning forward, his arms spread, the knife, a long-bladed stiletto, in his right hand.

'Come! Come!' He shouted. He drew closer. I could smell his cheap aftershave mingled with his sweat.

'Petro, get back to the ship! Go, now!'

'Not leaving you here, man,' he said, his voice still slurred.

'Just go! Tell the skipper what's happening. I can handle this. Go now!' Probably a mistake, I thought. But events were moving fast. The adrenalin was pumping and raw instinct was taking over from rational thought. I *did* believe I could handle it.

Petros began lurching down the street. Then he stopped and looked back. 'Just go!' I shouted and he turned and staggered on back towards the docks. He'd be more hindrance than help in a fight anyway, I figured.

The pimp used this diversion to lunge at me with the knife. I raised my forearm as a shield and the blade sliced through my sleeve. He slashed again, this time at my face. I pulled back and tried to grab the knife but the blade sliced the palm of my right hand, blood streaming from the cut. I was reacting, and it wasn't working. I needed to gain an advantage. I moved back until my back was against the wall. This time when he came at me I raised my foot and struck out, landing it hard against his knee. He screamed and backed away, off-balance for a moment. I moved in then and punched him in the solar plexus with my left. He reeled back, gasping for air. I waited until he'd pulled himself up, then aimed another blow at his jaw but connecting this time with his throat. He went backwards, clutching at his neck.

Stumbling over the kerb, he lost his footing and fell heavily into the road. I heard his head crack as it hit the cobbles. Then he lay still.

I leaned back against the wall, catching my breath and trying to make sense of what had just happened. Then I moved to where he lay and crouched down beside him, only to see his dead eyes staring straight back at me. I'd killed him.

A crowd had gathered, as they do in these situations. The fight had erupted and ended in no more than a couple of minutes yet there must have been twenty people gathered around me as I looked up. Now they were shouting – at me, at each other. I couldn't tell. I decided to stay where I was. To run or to try and explain what had happened seemed pointless. There were witnesses and the man's knife was still clutched in his hand with my blood on it.

But when the police arrived minutes later, gathering evidence from a crime scene was the last thing on their minds. I didn't understand a word of what was being said but the outcome was clear. I was handcuffed and placed under arrest. It was best this way, I told myself. Let justice take its course.

Aye, right.

Chapter 7

Riga–Daugavpils, Latvia

March 1999

For the first three days I was held in a cell at Riga's police headquarters. I was not ill-treated and an English-speaking policewoman was assigned to explain to me what was happening. The cut on my right hand was deep but had been cleaned, stitched and bandaged by a nurse they'd called in that first night. And I had been fed: borscht with a chunk of bread. Not bad under the circumstances, I thought. The policewoman said I'd be held until charges were brought against me. I didn't sleep that first night. Mostly I just paced up and down the small cell wondering how it had happened, how it could have been avoided and what the hell was going to happen next. Had the *Electra M* sailed? Had Christos Mavritis been informed? What kind of account had Petros given of the incident? Above it all hovered my fear that I'd be charged with murder.

On the fourth morning I was led to a grimy bathroom with a shower cubicle. The shower rattled while dispensing an intermittent spray of cold, brown water. I didn't linger. I asked about breakfast and was presented with a cup of hot, weak and strange-tasting coffee, but no food. I was then handcuffed again and taken to a room with a table and chairs.

Like everything else in the police station, the walls, floor and furniture were old and dilapidated.

An investigating judge appeared accompanied by his clerk and two police officers, the woman from the night before and an inspector. It was explained to me that the judge would perform an examining role and would be actively involved in the conduct of the investigation. I would be assigned a defence lawyer who would represent me, but not be responsible for investigating the case himself. That was the judge's role. Finally, the British embassy would be informed of my arrest. When I said I wanted my employers, the shipowner to be informed, they said that would be up to the embassy. Meanwhile I would be remanded without bail while charges were prepared.

And so it began. I was transferred in a police van stinking of sweat and urine to a prison many miles from Riga to await the outcome of the judge's investigation. I had no idea where it was, other than that it was inland, away from the port. This made me even more uncomfortable. Conditions here were much worse than at the police station. I quickly learned that it was known as White Swan, a romantic-sounding name for a prison that, as I also soon learned, was notorious for its often gratuitous maltreatment of prisoners, its gang culture among the inmates and its reputation for being impregnable. It was a once-white building dating back to the 1800s, and it looked like it hadn't been whitewashed since. There was a weathervane on the roof more or less in the shape of a swan. Eventually I was told the prison was located on the outskirts of a city called Daugavpils. But if the place itself looked grim from the outside, this was only a soothing introduction to what the inside was like.

On arrival I was taken to a room and strip-searched by two prison officers who must have weighed three hundred kilos between them. They stank of sweat too, but then by this time, so did I. Their uniforms were ill-fitting and didn't look particularly clean. They took my clothes and left me in the holding cell, which had nothing in it – nothing. I sat down in a corner, naked, shivering and wondering how much worse it was going to get.

Eventually, one of them brought me a pile of prison overalls. He waited while I dressed then handcuffed my hands, this time behind my back, and marched me down a corridor with cells either side from which emanated a disturbing range of shouts, cries and roars. I sensed some of the noise was directed at me, though I had no idea what was being said. We arrived at a cell into which I was pushed. The guard removed the handcuffs and left. The cell had two narrow beds separated by an aisle no more than three feet wide. A man was lying on one of them.

'Hi,' I said.

'What's your name?' the man asked, swinging his feet off the bed and standing up.

'Angus,' I said. 'Yours?'

'I am Maksims. You are English. I don't like English and I don't speak English language,' he said in passable English.

'Sorry about that. I'm Scottish.' I didn't think that would make any difference, and it didn't.

'Same thing.'

We left it like that. The cell, like the rest of the place, was filthy. The walls were peeling and covered with green mould. It smelled of mould, sweat and urine. I would never get used to these smells, however they were blended. The noise coming from outside continued: shouting and banging, the occasional scream. I lay down on the thin grubby mattress and tried to stop myself thinking – of anything.

The next day I was moved into a dormitory with five other men. It was never explained to me why, but I was glad to be shot of Maksims.

On the fifth day of my incarceration, I was taken to a room where a court-appointed defence lawyer presented himself. His English was somewhere between poor and incomprehensible. The embassy had been informed, he said, though he gave no indication as to if or when anyone might pay me a visit, despite my asking. He said the judge would be arriving shortly and he would wait with me until he arrived. He didn't want to discuss my case until the judge was present, he said, which struck me as odd.

The same judge I'd met in Riga reappeared and interviewed me. I told him the truth, in detail: my background, my occupation, the reason for my ship being in Riga. I told him that I had acted in self defence and that the man had lost his balance after I had struck him. I pointed out the injury to my hand and asked if the police had matched my blood to the knife my assailant had been carrying. And I asked him whether he was interviewing any of the numerous witnesses to the incident. Yes, he said, he had done these things.

'When will my case come before the court?' I asked.

'In due course,' he said.

On day twelve, a consular officer, who introduced himself as Dominic Farrington from the British embassy, came to see me. He said I could expect a fair trial but not to expect any leniency.

'Who is your next of kin?' he asked.

'I don't have a next of kin,' I answered, without going to the trouble of explaining that that person might or might not be a distant cousin, uncle or aunt who I'd never met. 'Has my employer been informed – the shipowner?'

'I believe so. But it's a little complicated. I understand the physical owner of the ship is located in Piraeus, while the registered owner is in Cyprus. And the ship itself is registered in Panama. And you are a British citizen. So you can appreciate there is little we can do on that front.'

'It's the physical owner I'm talking about – in Greece. His name is Christos Mavritis and I'm sure he knows what has happened and will do all he can to get me out of here. Would you ask the Greek embassy to assist please?'

'We have been in touch with our counterparts at the Greek embassy. They say they will be communicating with their colleagues in Athens on the matter. We'll no doubt be hearing from them in due course.'

'In due course!' I exploded. 'Is that something in your training manual under what to tell British citizens trapped in a shithole like this through no fault of their own? In due course?'

'There's no need to shout, Mr McKinnon. From what I know of your case, you became involved in a fracas which might well have been avoided by trying a little measured dialogue with the man you killed.'

I stared at him. Then, rashly perhaps, told him to fuck off.

As the days went by I spoke with other prisoners, some of whom were awaiting trial like myself. My mood would swing from one end of the spectrum to the other. At times I would feel quietly optimistic, trusting in the judicial process running its course to a fair conclusion, that being a verdict of innocence. At others, I would sink into black despair, convinced I'd be stuck in this stinking pit for years, or even, conceivably, face the death penalty.

It was on one of my darker days following the consular officer's visit that events took an unexpected turn. I was in the canteen for what passed as lunch – another bowl of tepid borscht with a lump of stale bread – when an elderly inmate sat down opposite me. I'd noticed him before; a gaunt man in his early sixties, I guessed. He had an intelligent face with large, watery eyes behind round-framed glasses. His skin was pallid and his wispy hair white. He smiled a listless smile and leaned across the table. 'You had a visit from your embassy? You are British, yes?'

'That's right,' I said, glad of someone to converse with in my own language.

'I believe you are a seafarer. Am I right?'

'Yes,' I said. By now this was common knowledge in our part of the prison. He reached across the table to shake my hand.

'I am Valdis,' he said, 'Valdis Ozols. I was sailor too – long time ago. I need your help, my friend.'

Chapter 8

Daugavpils, Latvia

March 1999

And so began a series of conversations, or monologues, often lasting hours at a time, with consequences I could never have foreseen. As the weeks went by my new friend revealed his life story and the dilemmas he now faced. But as my own trial loomed, with what looked more and more likely to be a long prison sentence, I was glad of the distraction his stories offered. We talked at meal times, in the prison laundry where, through his intervention, we were both assigned, and when any other opportunity presented itself. The more engrossed I became by this diversion, the less I obsessed about my own predicament, at least temporarily. I had tried several times to draw Valdis on why he was in gaol. What had he been convicted of, I asked but he was evasive, saying he would explain soon. The one thing he did reveal was that he had been working for British Intelligence for many years. It was enough to hold my attention.

I'd been in White Swan for only five weeks when my case came up, though it had seemed a lifetime. I was summoned to a local court and the trial began. There were no witnesses called, no jury, no members of the public, no journalists and no representative from the embassy present.

It lasted just over two hours. I was found guilty of manslaughter and, after another week, another eternity, was returned to the court to receive a sentence of nine years. I'd been expecting something like this by now, but that didn't lessen the shock. I felt physically sick as, handcuffed, I was escorted from the court building. Trees lining the edge of a small park displayed their bright green spring foliage, and beyond them I caught a glimpse of people sitting on the grass enjoying themselves, before I was shoved back into the van and back to the joys of White Swan.

The following day I was on laundry duty with Valdis. I told him my news. By this time, our friendship had evolved beyond just the casual companionship of two fellow inmates. Valdis's own mood had lifted noticeably in response to my presence – two fellow seafarers with many stories to share with one another. And he sensed my own mood, which had now changed from despair to a growing sense of anger and self-righteousness.

'Angus,' he said that morning as we piled dirty bed linen and towels into the decrepit old machines, 'you are upset.'

'I'm okay, really.' I took a deep breath. I was upset alright.

'You are sweating. You are cracking your knuckles. You just kicked laundry basket. Now I'm afraid you punch me or one of the guards to release emotions. And your Scottish voice stronger now than before. Calm down and listen to me. Angus, you are spark that has, how to say, lighted again fire inside me. Now I must do same for you. Words are not enough, I know. We need action, but I remember what my old friend Archie told me. He would say: "*Illegitimi non carborundum*". You know what it means?'

'I've no idea.'

He laughed. 'It is Latin. Roughly means don't let bastards break you down! British army intelligence used during war, he told me. Remember if it helps. It still helps me, and of course no one understands meaning. But yes, we need action, a plan, my friend. But first I continue my story, because only then will you understand what we must do.'

'Okay, but tell me first what you're doing in here.'

'Long story, I will tell you. I have been in here for eight months already. I am a prisoner of others inside this prison. All because of some very important information, some knowledge I have, but this will make no sense unless you hear my story from beginning.'

It began with his abduction by Archie, the Englishman, on that stormy night in Beirut, thirty-seven years earlier.

'I could not believe what was happening to me! I knew about Philby's defection of course. As ship's political officer

I was closely involved in last-minute plans to get him out of Beirut and on his way to Moscow. I came ashore with another crewman just as Philby arrived. It was a KGB plan but ever since I'd been assigned political officer position in Morflot, I was GRU man. Morflot was my employer but although Morflot reported to Ministry of Merchant Marine, it was also instrument of GRU when it came to intelligence matters. And we were in strong position to gather intelligence as our ships called at ports all over the world.

'So imagine my surprise! "Call me Archie", he would say after we had dropped formalities. Yes, we got on well. I knew now his name was Archie Anderson. He dropped alias when we were together during early days in Lebanon. But I understood risks I was taking, and that he was exposing me to. And when time came for the swap, that day at Crusader castle, I was frightened, I tell you. His plan was very risky. The swap worked, but once those GRU men had me then it was up to me to convince them that I had not been turned.

'We travelled north to Damascus in car. That fool Rybakov said he was to have pleasure of interrogating me. It was just a threat. It wasn't his job. He was a bully but he was not professional interrogator. Maybe it would have been better for me if he had done the questioning. A beating perhaps, a lot of shouting, yes, but Rybakov was not really interested in me. So I was driven to Aleppo and from there flown to Moscow.

'That's where the professionals were. They interrogated me for weeks in GRU headquarters on Prechistenka Street. At first they listen to my cover story, my legend as Archie called it, that the British tried to persuade me to spy for them as double agent but that I had refused. I told them that I had not been mistreated and in the end the British had accepted that my loyalty was with Soviet state. I told them I thought the British may have kidnapped me in Beirut just to swap me for British spy. I pretend not to know who, or much of anything, in case that make them suspicious. I was simple seaman. Only of course I was not simple seaman. I was political officer and double agent working for the British.' He glanced at me with a small smile.

'They tried hard to break me. In night they play loud music and switch light in cell on and off, on and off, over and over again. The questioning always be in middle of night. I was not allowed to sleep, and food was bad. Sometimes I would get nothing to eat for one or two days. Then something good would be brought to my cell, but just thrown off plate and onto floor. There was very small window high up on wall. That was only way I could tell whether it was night or day. I had no contact with anyone except the two interrogators. But sometimes, I would hear screams and moaning. And they were real screams. It terrified me. It still does.'

He shuddered involuntarily, then continued: 'They say it was alright to work for British, but I would still work for GRU, feeding lies back to London. They said I had been compromised, but they would forgive me and I could become redoubled agent for GRU – a triple. But seemed too good to be true. It would be like admitting being guilty, and even if I didn't get bullet in back of head right then, I would always be under their control.

'Archie said that nothing was expected until I was ready. "Go back to normal life," he said. "When you are cleared, and you will be, rebuild your career with Morflot at sea, then come ashore and find work, but try stay in shipping business. That's where your contacts will be. And only when you are ready will you make contact with us." It might take years, but he knew I was loyal to spy for Britain, for West.'

He talked about Cuba. 'Of course, my interrogators in Moscow knew all about Cuba. It was on their files. Even Delfina! Imagine how I feel when they say her name to me. They said I could go back to Cuba and see her if I agree to this position they plan for me. I didn't believe them. I did not trust them. But I knew, after what I saw in Cuba, that I had to play my part in preventing nuclear war, even if that meant betraying bastard Soviets. They were not my people. I am Latvian, not Soviet or Russian. And I tell you, after interrogation I was even more ready to work for British.'

Valdis wanted to tell his story as it had happened, so as his life unfolded before me I still had no idea what he was doing in gaol. It was 1999. We were approaching the new Millennium. The Soviet Union had collapsed a decade earlier and Latvia, following their Singing Revolution, was now an independent state, its application to join the European Union almost a done deal. Indeed, Latvia was by now well into its succession process in following the *acquis communautaire* route required of membership candidates. But this was now, not later, and the Soviet legacy hung heavy over its former satellites – and particularly over Latvia. As Valdis explained things to me, I realised how true this was.

I pressed him again: 'What are you doing in here, Valdis? You should be enjoying your retirement by now.'

'You notice three guys sit behind us in dining room?'

'Yes, I think so.'

'You have your back to them but I face them. They are GRU, I am telling you. We should stop sitting together.'

'What makes you so sure?'

'Believe me. I recognise them anywhere. For one thing, they don't communicate with other prisoners – at all. Second, guards leave them alone. You never see guards bothering them as they do with us and the others.'

'Maybe they're just gangsters who bribe the guards to treat them well. It doesn't make them GRU, surely?'

He laughed. 'If you spend most of your life as close to that organisation as I have, then you would understand. They are here to watch me. Makes sense. I explain everything later. It is too early now, but we must be careful. I don't want you to get involved. They are bad people. From now on we don't sit together and we try and mix more with other prisoners. Okay?'

'Sure, no worries. But are we safe from them here?' I gestured around the laundry room.

'For now, yes, safe. So now I must continue. We don't have much time.'

Having endured weeks of interrogation in Moscow, Valdis had been rehabilitated and sent back to sea, again as a political officer for Morflot. He would never be fully trusted by the GRU but they had bigger fish to fry than Valdis Ozols and he was granted conditional clearance.

'For next twelve years I continue my life as seafarer. Never promoted, just keep my job as third mate and political officer and I was good at my job, because I knew the GRU were keeping eye on me. Was obvious. So I had to take great care. Did not do much real spying for British for all those years. Of course, I send coded messages back on port activities that I thought may be useful, but I felt guilty I was not doing more for Archie. He treated me well and he hoped I would provide good intelligence – deeper intelligence. But risk was too great and I was afraid. I had heard a story from some of the other Morflot political officers. Still disturbs me today.'

'What was that?'

'I told you about Cuba and shipping those missiles. Well, what I did not tell you was that it was GRU man who helped stop that crisis turning into war. Was double agent called Oleg Penkovsky, worked for MI6. They were sharing their intelligence with CIA of course. Penkovsky provided much intelligence, including technical details about missile launch sites in Cuba. They say this gave Kennedy the information he needed to confront Khrushchev.'

'What happened to Penkovsky? Did he get caught?'

'Yes. Following year he was arrested, tried and executed.'

'Hardly surprising.'

'No, but how he was executed frightened me, even now it frightens me.'

'I thought it was a bullet in the back of the head for those kinds of crimes?'

'Not for Penkovsky. They tie him to stretcher and burn him alive in crematorium.'

'Jesus!'

'Meant as warning to others, GRU style. Make me afraid of fire, Angus.'

'But you still went ahead and spied against them.'

'Yes, but only after many years, because something happened. I will tell you.'

No sooner had he spoken than a prison guard came into the laundry. He began shouting at Valdis who just stood impassively, politely answering the man's staccato questions.

'What was all that about?' I asked when he'd stormed out.

'I complained about machines.' He gestured at the old hulks around us. 'Half of them are broken and the rest are rusty inside. They are shit. He says not for prisoner to complain and anyway we talk too much. He says he could send us to work in other part of prison.'

'Where?'

'The latrines. Don't worry, it was just threat because I complain. Not up to him to reassign anyone anywhere, but we must be careful. Let us continue tomorrow. Enough for one day, eh?'

Chapter 9

Daugavpils, Latvia

April 1999

'So where was I? Ah, yes, 1975.'

We were back in the laundry room. I was getting increasingly nervous about our meetings, but Valdis was persistent. He spoke more urgently now, determined to tell his story before jumping forward to the real purpose of our collaboration. 'I cannot tell you what is all about if you don't understand background. Please understand, yes?' he would say.

And I always did say yes. It didn't really matter I told myself, and if I was going to be in there for nine years, it helped pass the time. But there was something else besides relief from the hopeless boredom we endured and the sense of life passing me by. I needed to find out how he thought I could help him, and maybe help myself too.

'I was serving on ship of Latvian Shipping Company. Managed by Morflot, of course. They manage all merchant fleets in Soviet Union – Latvian, Estonian, Ukrainian. We were chartered to FESCO, Far Eastern Shipping Company, which operated liner service out of Nakhodka and Vladivostok calling at ports all around Far East. It was good run. We would be in port many days, sometimes a week or two. And usually allowed shore leave – good for crew and good for me – I could send messages to London, by dead drops.

'Then something happened. Was September '75. We were eastbound from Hai Phong. Yes, same port you sailed from, my friend. But we were bound for Makassar in Celebes. Our course took us across Sulu Sea. Was very beautiful. Calm waters after South China Sea. Sea was blue like sky, forests on islands green like emerald, beaches white. Little outrigger boats skim about all over place, sails bright with many colours: yellow, brown, green/blue, and stripes too. So beautiful.'

He smiled, reminded of his memories. 'I remember so well. When darkness comes on our second night in those waters, I watch light from algae in water, you know? It all shone in ship's wake and I think this must be most beautiful, peaceful place in world. Hah! I was wrong.

'Now remember, yes, I was political officer but also, as third mate I had watchkeeping duties and that night I was on middle watch, midnight to 0400 – you know, graveyard watch.

'I saw boats at 0215. I log them as fishing craft, one off our starboard bow, other to port. We saw they were closing on us but didn't know what it meant. Pirate attack against big, fast merchant ship like ours? Never. So not ready for what happened. There was rope holding two fishing boats together – but we didn't see it. How could we? They moved in way of our heading so when we approach the rope caught on bow of our ship – it—' he broke off to gesture the bulbous bow, looking to see I understood. I nodded quickly. '— it pulled each small fishing boat back and alongside us, either side of ship. We still not understand. Did they need help? We must assist mariners in distress – you know. Duty as old as man going to sea. Of course we would assist poor fishermen. I called captain. He was not happy being woken up but in five minutes he was on bridge. I was on starboard bridge wing and could see, even in darkness, three or four men climbing up ship's side! They throw grappling hooks up over ship's rail. They were boarding our ship!

'I go back into wheelhouse. The helmsman – he was young – had left the wheel and gone out onto port bridge wing. I hear him shout: "They're armed! Take cover!" Those were last words he spoke. Burst of shooting. I saw him thrown back onto deck. I ran out to him, keeping down low. Shooting almost take his head off. He was eighteen years.' As Valdis relived the moment, he spoke faster, the memories clearly as fresh and traumatic as if they'd happened yesterday. His English – usually not bad – became more erratic, but the story that unfolded was grimly clear.

'In few minutes they take control of ship. They tell us sail to anchorage long way off Jolo Island. First thing they do when we anchor is force chief mate to walk plank! They rig gangway, force him along, then push him off. "This is what we will do. Plenty sharks down there. Hope he drown before they get him!" their leader shout, laughing and pointing down at beautiful calm blue sea. Then one of others fire at the mate in water and sea goes dark where blood spread around his body. They laugh. They call their leader Amir. He spoke some English, but no Russian of course. He said they would keep captain alive to negotiate ransom payment so they had thrown mate overboard as warning to us all. They were pirate men, very well armed with automatic rifles and handguns too. Very violent guys.'

A quarter of a century later, Valdis could still barely tell the story, his voice now a hoarse whisper as he forced himself on. 'They wanted million dollars, for God's sake!

'We told them Soviet Union does not pay ransoms, so they threaten us more. In the end I told this Amir that maybe I could get them some ransom money. You see my position! I knew our own people would not pay a rouble. Even if captain had time to contact Vladivostok he would be told cannot expect assistance. And we knew Russian Navy had no ships in that region. If there were we would have known already. It was part of protocol for us to be told. So I persuade pirates to take me ashore if they want money. Only me.

'We go on board one of their little boats and head for coast. It took over an hour. There was small village behind beach where we landed. Just a few wooden huts with palm leaf roofs – *attap*, they call it. People came out to stare at us, but no one said anything. They looked frightened. We drove in old pick-up truck to another village, another hour travelling. In this village there was shack with phone. This whole time they had their guns on me, and I tell you, they were trigger happy.

'I called number Archie gave me many years ago, only to be used in emergency. My hands are shaking and I have to dial twice. But I get through – and then get transferred to another phone. I thought my heart would come through my chest, Angus! A woman answered the phone. Was his wife. She put me through and I spoke to him in Russian, so pirates think I'm talking to my bosses – lucky they don't understand, eh! I ask him if he can help. He ask where I am and what happened. Really, I expect him to say he can't do anything, but he just told me call back in two hours. Then I waited, promised pirates I could help them now. It was longest two hours of my life. Amir got very nervous. He kept asking me who I had spoken to and what was going to happen. Then Archie phoned, and he says he can help but I must prepare my crew for action without letting pirates know. "Tell them we will drop ransom from aircraft sealed in rubber bags with flotation chambers," he said, and after I told him exact coordinates where we were anchored, I asked him what would happen, but he just told me to be ready and to be alert.'

Valdis was on his feet, pacing up and down the laundry room, pausing to gesticulate at me in his vehemence. 'I told Amir how ransom money would be dropped from aircraft,' he continued. 'He said this to his gang and there was plenty of shouting and laughing. Amir fired his AK-47 in the air. They were crazy guys. We returned to the ship and I told captain to stand by and I had told my contacts in GRU. He wanted to know more but as political officer I outranked him in such matters, so I just told him be prepared for whatever might be coming. We discuss about a rescue but I didn't know, so couldn't tell him any more than that.

'We wait. Pirates tell us they will start killing us, one by one, if they don't see money coming. They were beginning to not believe my promise, and I was beginning to lose hope myself, but I kept telling them: "Soon you will be rich men", and that would make them excited. They were simple men but that didn't mean they were not dangerous. They had moved the whole crew into the messroom where they could guard us. We were crew of thirty-six men. Tensions were very high on both sides, them and us. Many times they would hit anyone who questioned or tried to argue with them. They used the butts of their rifles. We soon learned to keep quiet and keep our heads down. Time went so slowly. The cook fed the pirates and us, but we didn't eat much and only slept for short times.

'Finally – just after midnight on fourth day – hell break loose without warning. The noise! Grenades exploding. And there was all the time firing from automatic weapons. Before we knew it, men with masks burst into messroom where we were held.

'It was all over in less than ten minutes. I hadn't been told what to expect. I knew this raid was likely but hadn't told my shipmates. I didn't want them to get excited and alert the pirates. Now we ducked down and hid as best we could. But by then the pirates had all been dealt with – killed. They were easy to identify – dark, skinny and they were the only ones wearing balaclavas! There were seven of them and they didn't stand a chance. It was massacre, both out on deck where some of the pirates had rushed out to fight, and in messroom where others were guarding us.

'One of masked soldiers asked for captain. He talked to him in Russian, not fluent but not bad. Definitely a foreigner. He asked if our ship was seaworthy and ready to continue voyage. The captain said yes, she was. "Then do so," he said. "We shall escort you from a distance." And that was it. They were gone before anyone could ask questions. The engineers restarted main engine, we raised anchor and proceeded on our passage to Makassar. We never saw our escort. Captain asked me who had carried out the rescue. I told him I guessed it was Spetsnaz team from GRU but I had not been told. It was just a hunch, I said. He never questioned the foreign-sounding Russian accent. He was glad just to be free. We all were. We were shouting with joy, and the vodka came out. Of course, I believed it was the Royal Navy Marines. I was never told the full story. The British Intelligence agencies like to keep their operations in separate boxes, separate rooms. I learned this later. It makes sense. Only much later the Admiral told me it was Special Boat Service.'

'Who's the Admiral?' I asked as I absorbed this extraordinary tale.

'Later. Later I will tell you who he is.'

'So what was the upshot of it all?'

'We got rid of bodies, cleaned up ship and weeks later returned to Nakhodka and carried on our liner service. But orders were issued to bypass Sulu Sea.' Valdis was calmer now, speaking more slowly and coherently. I could tell the next part of his story had been safely processed into the past, unlike the attack from the pirates.

'My bosses became suspicious, never mind that I had saved crew and ship. The captain was questioned by the Morflot people. I was too of course, but I kept to my story – that my phone calls had been to contacts in GRU so they should talk to them if they wanted answers. Who did I speak to, they asked? I said I couldn't tell them. It was risky but I hid behind secret cloak of GRU, which was, still is an organisation to be afraid of. And it was not Morflot's job to start looking into GRU business. I knew there would be people who had suspicions, but most of Morflot management people were very pleased and they knew better than to ask questions. It was Soviet way: you knew how far it was safe to go, and Morflot demanding details about covert GRU operations was step too far.'

'Were you not rewarded for saving the lives of your crew?'

'No, and I didn't mind that. My shipmates and Morflot colleagues appreciated what I had done and I didn't want to draw more attention to myself. Anyway, after that my sea career was soon over and I was sent to my hometown of Ventspils, which suited me very well. I was given job in harbourmaster's office and I lay low there. I met beautiful girl. We married and we had a daughter.'

'Where are they now, Valdis?'

'My wife died some years ago. She had stroke and was paralysed. She lived for two years and then I think she gave up. My heart was broken. My daughter works in Vienna now. She is scientist, still training. But I must continue with my story, then you can ask me as many questions as you like.'

'Valdis, you have my full attention. What else are we going to do in this hellhole?'

Chapter 10

Daugavpils, Latvia

April 1999

Valdis wanted to share all his experiences. It wasn't just about my having to understand the background, there was more to it than that. He also needed to share a burden. He said he needed my help, but had still not explained what he expected from me. But the story he'd just told was so gripping that for a while I'd escaped from White Swan and was with him and his shipmates on that azure blue sea.

'I must tell you how happy I am to share my life here with you, my dear friend.' Valdis was in a buoyant mood induced by his recollections. It wasn't always easy, but when one of us was down, the other usually managed to lift his spirits.

'So, after incident in Sulu Sea, when I was settling into new job ashore, I received a signal.'

'What kind of signal?' I'd resigned myself to having to make these interruptions as he tended to assume that I would know how his secretive line of work actually functioned in practice.

'Ha! I cannot give you details of all the tradecraft they taught and set up for me, but the signal told me to meet my handler at Kronvalda Park in Riga. I took time off work, travelled to Riga and went to park as instructed. There, sitting on park bench, was my old friend Archie Anderson! I couldn't believe it. I was worried to be meeting him in the open like that, but we had both taken precautions to ensure we were not followed or watched. It was winter, it was raining and of course, he had an umbrella. There were very few people about, which made me cautious and nervous. I had seen a woman sitting on nearby bench. She had pushchair and was talking to baby or small child. You know, the way that mothers do, but in the rain? I mentioned it to Archie. He said she was wife of one of their people at the embassy and was there to keep eye open for anyone acting suspiciously. She would alert us with prearranged signal, but I don't know how useful she really was.'

'So, what did he want?'

'We talked of many things, but main reason for his visit was to tell me he was retiring. I was alarmed! I had grown to trust him and although we had not met very often in all those years, I relied on him to look after me and my family if things ever got very difficult – if we would ever have to leave this country in hurry. He told me not to worry, but that my case was being transferred to another department and I was to be assigned new case officer. It had been decided in London that all their agents in Eastern Bloc who had maritime connections, and especially those like me with GRU connections as well, were to be handled by Defence Intelligence, not MI6. My new handler was a rear admiral. He was from Naval Intelligence, which had been merged with other military intelligence agencies back in 1960s. This I knew.

'And Archie told me something else: that the operation to free our ship in Sulu Sea, and for which I thanked him of course, had been planned and run by this same rear admiral. He had even been on board Royal Navy destroyer from which raiding party had been sent and which shadowed us as we continued our voyage to Makassar.'

'So who is this rear admiral?'

'Ha! No names, no pack-drill. That was one of Archie's sayings. I never understood where it came from. He was full of old English sayings I had never learned when studying English. But I can only tell you Archie's name because it is in public domain. He is even writing autobiography, would you believe this, so I know his name but not admiral's name. All I know is that he operates from unit in British Defence Intelligence. International Maritime Task Force. Was set up to fight maritime terrorism and piracy. That is why they were effective with raid in Sulu Sea. They work with British Special Forces. IMTF carries out investigation, then works with Royal Marines or Special Boat Service for planning and execution. Even with SAS sometimes. IMTF is small department. No big network of agents. Just use NOCs – I mean non-official cover, sometimes marine investigators, MI6, Special Forces, whoever needed for the job.

'So that day in park Archie wanted to say goodbye and tell me how things would work in future. He knew I was more or less sleeper since I had come ashore. Even when I was at sea I was only passing routine intel reports back to London from whatever port I could. That depended on case officer being available, which wasn't always possible. For example, in Hong Kong it worked. In Makassar, forget it! I had to wait until we reached a port where there was British embassy or consulate and dead-drop arrangements would be made there.

'But all was going to change now, he said. London was worried about Soviet missile sites being established in Baltic states at that time, especially in Latvia: the Dvina missile silo had four launchers for R-12 ballistic missiles. Such missiles could attack targets at a range of thousands of kilometres. The radars in Skrunda-1 town in western Latvia covered the airspace of all Western Europe. They could detect any launch of ballistic missile from that area. Remember, all this was in middle of '70s. It is just ghost town now. Then there was Zeltini Nuclear Missile Base in north-east of country. Now you can visit it as tourist if you want. Would you believe it?'

'Valdis, I don't want to visit it as a tourist. No offence, but I want to get out of Latvia and never come back! Why are you telling me all this stuff?' I was getting uncomfortable again about these sensitive disclosures, even if the Soviet Union was dead and gone.

'Because you need to understand full story if you are to help me. Please, Angus, be patient a little longer and everything will become clear, I promise. And do not let your attention leave you! So, to continue, Zeltini storage and launch complex was originally built for 2.3 megaton single-warhead nuclear missile. But also kept there was smaller SS-21 Scarab, or what the Soviets called Tochka missile. Can fire 100 kiloton nuclear warhead distance of 185 kilometres. It is tactical weapon for use on battlefield. Short range.'

'These names and numbers mean nothing to me,' I said impatiently.

'Listen to me! Missile system – same system sent to Cuba in 1962 – did not have extra range needed to reach targets in Europe from faraway in Russia. This made Baltic region very interesting to Soviet military, and that is why Zeltini was built and was updated and kept in active state until end of Soviet Union and withdrawal of Red Army back to Russia. And of course they carried away all those weapons with them. Or we thought they did.

'Then, that day in park, Archie says they want me to start investigating these sites. By "they" he means Admiral's IMTF. At first I was worried about undertaking such dangerous work, but he told me, relax. He was good at that and I knew I would miss his words of encouragement. He was kind man. He had good English sense of humour too. But sitting there on bench that day in rain and feeling worried, I had to remind myself, this was what I had always wanted, ever since Cuba: to play my part in nuclear disarmament.

'But there was more. They needed to know about what Twice Red-Banner Baltic Fleet. This supported northern flank of European theatre in case of confrontation with NATO. This was very valuable strategically and if war broke out, this fleet would be carrying out amphibious assaults against the coasts of Denmark and Germany. I knew now my time had come. The intelligence gathering I had been doing so far was small potato. Now serious work would begin. And I was ready. So we said goodbye there in park and I returned to Ventspils feeling sad to be saying goodbye to an old friend, and a little excited and afraid – all at once. It was very emotional day for me.'

'So what happened? Did you find what they wanted?'

'Finding information on Twice Red Banner Baltic fleet was not so difficult for me. I had access through my work, you know. But missile sites were different matter. I used my job as assistant harbourmaster to get information, and this is important to what I tell you shortly. Morflot fleet was used to ship military equipment, including missiles, and they used Latvian ports like Ventspils. So I could ask questions without going near GRU. And my new masters, IMTF, had clever ways for me to transfer this intelligence without arousing suspicion.' He laughed. '"Let's keep it simple", they would say. And we did. A British shipping line would call at Ventspils every two weeks in those days. It was routine for me to visit the ships when they called, so no problem for me to pass envelope to captain. And captain had been briefed by Admiral's people. Easy!'

I'd listened for hours, days to his story. I liked the man and I felt sorry for him. His health was poor, he was widowed. His daughter lived in another country and it seemed he was afraid for his life. And his stories were enthralling, saving us both from losing our minds; but he still hadn't told me what he was doing in that dreadful place, or what he wanted from me. Finally though, when he'd brought his tales of espionage up to date and I'd pressed him once again, his present troubles began to emerge. And I quickly realised they were inextricably linked to my own.

Chapter 11

Daugavpils, Latvia

April/May 1999

'I had freed myself from GRU, or I thought I had.' Valdis was continuing his story some days later, and again we were in the laundry room. 'Then everything changed, at first for better. USSR collapsed! Who could ever have thought it would happen? But it did – suddenly! Imagine! We - my wife, my daughter and myself, we formed part of human chain from Estonia, across Latvia and across Lithuania: Singing Revolution it was called. We began to demand for restoration of Latvia's independence. We reclaimed sovereignty and eventually we gained independence. Now we are close to joining you in European Union. We could never have dreamt of it. And now my daughter has good job, career in EU country.'

'Who does she work for in Vienna?' I asked.

'I am proudest of fathers. She studied at the Jāzeps Vītols Latvian Academy of Music in Riga. She is talented pianist but in such competitive world and I cannot give more money for musical education, she changed her plan and now studies nuclear physics at the Atominstitut in Vienna. This is internship with International Atomic Energy Agency. Brilliant girl, and still so young. She inherited her brains from her mother, not from me. And in Vienna she is able to follow her love of music, of course. She makes recitals. Much appreciated by audience.'

At first he smiled and his face took on an indulgent expression I hadn't seen before. 'I love her so much,' he said, gazing off into the middle distance. 'One day you have daughter, you will understand.' Then he began to cry, quietly. He buried his head in his hands and groaned softly. 'Oh, what can I do? What can I do?'

'Tell me!' I shouted above the sound of the laundry machines. I wanted to help and I hated seeing the old man so upset. 'What is it you're not telling me?'

He looked up at me and composed himself. 'I am sorry, Angus. Truly, and now it is time for you to know, if we are to help each other.'

At last, I thought.

'I am here not because I have committed crime, not against Latvian state anyway. As I told you before, I am here because of GRU's influence. They are responsible for it. Remember, in Latvia today over 30 per cent of population is still Russian. Many of those Russians are still connected to old state apparatus – especially military, and therefore to GRU. Ever since collapse of Soviet state there has been much chaos. You know this. The military has been part of this chaos and so has GRU. And in a world of chaos there lie many opportunities for criminal and very profitable activities … You know about loose nukes, yes?'

'No.'

'It is what Americans call nuclear weapons that cannot be accounted for. Many have been identified and secured, but some have not. I know these things because I was monitoring them for the Admiral. Remember Cuban missile crisis. How did those missiles reach Cuba? By sea of course, on ships from the same class as my old friend *Dolmatova*. Those Morflot ships carried the missiles from ports like Ventspils – my port.

'So, just nine months ago, nuclear weapon from Zeltini goes missing. I know many people who work at Zeltini. When missiles or nuclear materials are moved in and out, always come through my port, Ventspils. So I handle all logistics, all documents, and I liaise with them.

'I have good idea who took it: who transported it to Ventspils, then exported it on ship belonging to Latvian shipowner. All illegal of course. No documents, no authorisation. They must have had help from inside. There was much talking about it at Zeltini, of course. They told me the fools had taken the missile but not the launch code! This made me think, the Admiral would find this very interesting, and what if I could get the launch code? Maybe it will help to track the missile and the people who stole it. They will need the code, so maybe we can draw them to us.

'But how to get the code? So, you must understand that the men and women who work at Zeltini have become rather careless since Soviets left. And the whole base is due to be closed down anyway. They do not like their jobs. They are not well paid and they have other work – black market work. I could not risk bribing them, but I did learn where the launch codes were kept for all missiles there – in a safe. But I did not need to steal it.'

'What do you mean?'

'Ha! I had seen where the combination numbers for the safe were kept: in the drawer of a desk nearby to safe. On computer printout. Would you believe this? One afternoon – day after I heard of missile stolen – I took vodka and some nice food: shashlik, smoked fish, even caviar for the two men who worked in that department where safe was. I knew them. They were bachelors, I was widower. We talked and had good times together. It was summer. I had opened window and they didn't close it when we left; they were drunk. That night I came back. I knew perimeter fence was broken. And if foxes and, how do you say, jenotsun – racoon dog, and other animals could get under fence, then so could I. Then climbed through window. It was hardest part for me, and coming back through window too. But into safe was easy. I memorised code – not so difficult, only eight digits. And now I know how to launch that missile. And that makes things dangerous for me, you see?'

I did see. 'So you mean this Tochka has been shipped out of the country? Where has it gone?'

'I don't know. I can tell you there is just one missile, that I know of anyway, armed with nuclear warhead and mounted on launcher. But where it has gone, I do not know. Ship sailed and declared Rotterdam anchorage for orders. I know this but it means nothing.'

'Why didn't you pass this information back to London?'

'How could I when I was locked up here?'

'So who exactly kidnapped you?'

'Day after I took launch code, I left from harbourmaster's office on way home. It was dark. I was careless – always walked same route home, same time. Stupid. Every day I told myself must walk another way home. That night I had some vodkas, by myself in the office. I was little bit drunk. Live alone now. Wife gone, daughter gone. I planned to pass intel back to London same night but GRU guys come in car, stopped ahead of me on quiet street and caught me. Simple. Injection, then next thing I am here. No trial, no lawyer, no Admiral. Only you.

'So that is situation. What to do? I must contact Admiral, but how? That is why I need you, my friend. You have contact with your embassy and through that contact we can reach Admiral. But we must hurry! How long before they take me away from here? They must know I have code. That is why they kidnap me. They are just holding me here, for now. Look, I have been around these people for so many years. I know them and I know their methods. When I say 'rogue' I don't mean they do not have contacts in the official GRU. Of course they do. That is how things work in Former Soviet Union these days.'

'Right, so what do they plan to do with it? Who's their enemy?'

'No, no. They plan to sell it. Or perhaps they have already sold it. I don't know.'

'Who buys these things? Terrorists?'

'Yes, eventually. But I believe there may be middle men involved. Not just brokers but other buyers and sellers – traders. It is, opaque. Archie liked that word. Opacity: it defines the world he and I worked in, he would say.'

'So, you want me to persuade a British embassy man to call round here for a chat. I can try but I'll need a good pretext to convince them I'm not wasting their time. They haven't been very sympathetic to my plight so far.'

'Yes, but I have no way myself of contacting Admiral. I cannot just ask to see man from British embassy. And Admiral has no way of knowing what has happened to me, where I am. I was taken off street and hidden away here. But you have access, and that is how you can help me. Admiral can help us both. That must be our purpose: to get out of here, both of us.'

'So this GRU gang must have a lot of influence.'

'Influence through this,' he said rubbing his thumb against his fingers. 'You buy influence and favours in this country nowadays, in dollars.'

'And they are keeping you here to prevent you informing your British masters of this theft of the missile? Do they have any evidence that you're working for the British? If I'm to meet the Admiral I must know these things.'

'Not for sure, just strong suspicion. Remember: my file, my record. They have good reasons to suspect me, if not that I already passed intelligence to London, then just that I knew about this stealing of missile because of my work as harbourmaster at Ventspils port. That is enough for them to keep me silent. There is more: even though I am almost retired, I still have contacts, friends I keep in touch with, for good reasons you understand. They put this together with my record already over so many years – Cuba, the Sulu Sea

– all is on my record, and maybe things I don't know of. All is enough for them to distrust me and have me locked up here. This is safe place to keep me. And think of it. If you are trading nuclear weapons you cannot afford to take chances. A suspicion is enough for them. It is lucky I am still alive.'

'And you think they know you have the code.'

'They must. Why else keep me in here. I might be very useful to them one day. I am like red flashing button: you can use me to launch missile. They do not have the code and not easy for them to get it.'

'I'm surprised they haven't tried to force it out of you already.'

'This is my fear. Maybe they will. Tomorrow, next day, tonight? This is why we must get out of here.'

'Why tell me this now. You should have said before, before you gave me all the back story.'

'Because they have just replaced GRU guys with three new ones. Maybe they are here to do it. I don't know.'

Chapter 12

Daugavpils, Latvia

May 1999

Gaining access to the consular officer was not as straightforward as the British Foreign Office pretended. Persons in custody who are citizens of the United Kingdom have the unrestricted right to receive visits from consular officers of their countries of nationality, it claimed. All visits must be requested in writing from the prison administration in good time, it said. I dutifully wrote a request and presented it to one of the guards who regularly patrolled our block. He looked at it, smiled and tore it up. 'Don't understand English,' he announced and walked away. I persisted, protesting to him each time until, after three days and three more written requests torn up, I collared a more senior guard who was doing the rounds and who I knew spoke more English. I had a fourth written request in my pocket and gave it to him, asking him if he could get the message to the British embassy for me. He looked at me, took the note, looked at it and walked off without saying a word.

'Will you?' I called after him. No response. I had to just wait and hope.

It was another three weeks before the consular officer finally appeared marking the end of my second month in

White Swan. It was the same character who had come before: Dominic Farrington. I began by apologising for my outburst at our previous meeting, a gesture which he studiously disregarded. This meeting took place across a table in a room I hadn't been in before. A guard stood in the corner. He looked bored, gazing around him as if impatient for us to get finished. I took this as a good sign. I had a better chance of getting my message across if the guard wasn't paying attention. I spoke quickly and quietly while trying to avoid appearing furtive. 'This is extremely important,' I said. 'You must get word to the Ministry of Defence, to the Admiral in charge of the International Maritime Task Force. Do you understand?'

He was young and his manner had been condescending up to this point. To him I was a low-life sailor who'd brought his fate upon himself. He knew my case but still acted like he'd rather be somewhere other than in this dump. And I wouldn't argue with that, but I had his attention now.

'Go ahead,' he said cautiously, moving a little closer across the table.

'Tell them that Humming Bird is here. He was snatched off the street nine or ten months ago. He has vital information about the theft of a nuclear warhead and his life is in danger. He is under the guard of the GRU, or a rogue element of the GRU, here in the prison. They've planted three of their thugs to keep an eye on him. He needs to get out and he needs the Admiral's help. Nuclear weapons are out there being traded and Humming Bird can help find them. This is a grave and precarious situation. He has asked me to act as go-between. It is extremely urgent. That's it. Visit me again when you have news.'

'Who is this Humming Bird?'

'Humming Bird is a codename. You don't need to know more than that. The Admiral will know who he is. Now just tell me you'll do it.'

'I'll see it's done,' he muttered hesitantly. 'There are people at the embassy …'

I'd told him enough for him to know I wasn't making it up as some kind of stunt and even if he did, he knew he couldn't afford to ignore it. I got up and nodded to the guard. Farrington stood too, looking awkward. The meeting was over.

When I got back to the laundry room, Valdis was waiting, nervously glancing around as he asked how the meeting had gone.

'He got the message and agreed to pass it on. Calm down, Valdis. We must wait now.' But I could see the paranoia mounting.

'I have asked if I can be in same dormitory with you. It will be safer if you are around.'

'What did they say to that? Surely you don't want to arouse even more suspicion.'

'No, don't worry. They know I am not a difficult prisoner, not violent. They said it could be arranged. I told them you wanted to learn our language and I would teach you. They liked that. It will be good on your record too.'

'What about the triplets, your GRU goons?'

'They don't frighten me,' he said. Maybe not, I thought, but they frightened me.

The arrival of the warmer days of summer was bittersweet. The days were longer but the birds sang less now than in the spring nesting season. I'd come to appreciate birdsong as a novelty. Besides the cry of gulls and other seabirds, the sounds of nature's creatures were largely absent at sea. The rats were an exception. The birdsong I heard from the confines of the prison represented freedom and joyfulness. It instilled a sense of hope. Now it was replaced by sounds of laughter and shouting from the surrounding streets out beyond the exercise yard, beyond the razor wire, as people were out and about enjoying the good weather. Birdsong, being non-human, was abstract. But human voices worked negatively on my mood only serving to remind me of my predicament. I was only a couple of months, or was it three now, into my nine-year sentence. When I thought about it, a rising sense of panic would envelop me. It was how I imagined drowning would be. The sense of optimism following my meeting with Farrington hadn't lasted. Valdis and I were sharing a dormitory with others from our caste now, and that had helped for a while, but Valdis's unrelenting paranoia was beginning to get to me. 'Just because I am paranoid doesn't mean they are not after me,' he would say only half humorously, claiming it was what had kept him alive all these years. I wondered who he'd picked that one up from. But if I'd thought he was imagining things, I was wrong, as events were to prove.

There are three castes in the Latvian prison hierarchy, and I had learned this pretty much from my first day there. *Blatnije*, meaning a favour for a favour, were the VIPs. *Mužiki* suggested someone is a true man, and these were your average thugs. And then there was the *Kreisie*, or the left, as in left behind. These were the bottom feeders. The average thugs are subservient to the VIP caste. If they don't accept this status they get booted down to the bottom-feeder level. The bottom feeders have no choice but to serve the thugs, who use them for their own purposes. The VIP prisoners don't ever speak to or use the same utilities as bottom feeders. This prison hierarchy is a structure created by the prisoners themselves and based on a sense of justice, a set of values, or so it was said. The prison authorities accepted this status quo. They didn't seem to have much choice in the matter.

Paedophiles, rapists and the most brutal murderers are automatically deemed bottom feeders and they are kept in separate cells for their own safety. But prisoners can be kicked down to the bottom feeder tier for even menial reasons like gambling debts or stealing food from other inmates. Such relegations are decided by the VIPs.

Valdis and I had been classed as *Mužiki.* Unfortunately, the GRU guys, Aramis, Athos and Porthos as Valdis had christened them in a futile attempt at comedy, were ranked as VIPs. Although us *Mužiki* did not share facilities with the VIPs, that didn't stop the GRU triplets entering the shower block when Valdis was in there one morning. Prisoners are often at their most vulnerable in the showers and Valdis was elderly and in poor health. The courage he'd shown for so many years as a double agent seemed to have deserted him, not because he was a coward, far from it, but because he was old enough and wise enough to know that he was vulnerable.

There were some very tough, violent men in that prison and some very unpleasant things went on in the shower block. Men were sodomised regularly and one young prisoner had been knifed to death a few days before Valdis encountered his own trouble there. He came back to the dormitory cell, bent over, holding his broken glasses, a towel tied round his waist, his wispy grey hair plastered to his skull; and he was shaking. I'd been in the shower block just before him and seen nothing other than the usual shouted threats and abusive language.

'What's wrong, Valdis? Sit down. Tell me.'

He sat on the edge of his bed. 'I knew it. I told you. They know who I am and now they want me to know that they know.'

'Did they hurt you?'

'First they threaten me. Then they hit me here.' He twisted painfully to show me where they'd punched him in the kidney on his right side. It was red and would darken into a bruise. 'They pushed me against the wall when I was in the shower. All three of them were there – naked. "Better watch it old man," they said. "We know all about you."'

'That doesn't necessarily make them GRU does it?' I asked, still not wanting to believe that the highly secret and notoriously brutal Russian military intelligence service was breathing heavily down our necks. 'Maybe they're just VIP gangsters having some fun at your expense. They're bullies, and bullies are cowards, so they pick on an old guy like you. Do you want me to lean on them?' I added, without feeling any confidence in what the outcome of that might be.

'No. Don't do that. I am just telling you. Believe me, they're not just bullies. I've told you this before. They are GRU bullies, or at least hired by the GRU. And I'm sure they are being well paid. I've heard of similar cases where prisoners are watched by GRU on the inside, but usually it's the guards or the warden who are hired to do the watching and report back.

'I said to them, who are you? They say: "Never mind, but remember you are safer in here than outside. In here you can do no harm. Out there, maybe you want to sing like a little bird. That would not be good for you. Not good at all." They wanted me to know that they have control of me in here and that they know my case. And if you want to believe they are just gangsters then you would never make a good spy, because a good spy is always suspicious. Always!'

'Then perhaps you should suspect me. I might be a plant. Anyway, I don't want to be a spy. I don't have the same reasons, the same cause, as you had.'

Eventually he calmed down – for a while. Then his impatience resurfaced: 'How long? How long before the Admiral comes? We need him, don't you understand?'

Chapter 13

Daugavpils, Latvia

May 1999

During our clandestine exchanges Valdis and I had spent time discussing ways and means of escape. These had ranged from digging tunnels, crawling along ventilation shafts or setting fires and initiating a mass breakout. Whichever option we chose, in the end we would always turn back to one imperative: the need for inside help.

Janis Berzins was the head guard assigned to G Block, where we were housed. My case was well known to all the guards. I'd killed a pimp in a fight. I even enjoyed kudos among some of the prisoners as details of my crime leaked out. Valdis, on the other hand, was a mystery man. No one was quite sure why he was there. To use his word, the charges were opaque. Certainly, except for the three GRU heavies, no one suspected he was a spy. But Berzins, Valdis and myself all shared one thing in common: we were seafarers – past or present. And through that common background we had formed a bond.

In White Swan there were around two hundred prisoners to each head guard. He had a number of assistants, who received only slightly better treatment from their boss than the prisoners themselves. Discipline was based largely on the caste system. Harsh though that regime was, in the absence of any effective control from the prison administration, it did work, in its own way.

Our relationship with Berzins made our lives a little easier. He was a man in his middle forties, had served with the same Morflot fleet as Valdis, but as a senior rating in the engineroom, and had come ashore in the hope that, following independence and the prospect of Latvia's EU membership, things could only get better. Only in the Latvian prison system where Soviet-era practices still prevailed, things weren't getting better at all.

Berzins spoke some English too. He had met plenty of Greeks, Indians and Filipinos in his seafaring days and, like most sailors, took an internationalist view towards mankind and the world around him. Valdis, and after a while myself too, cultivated what had become a furtive but nevertheless genuine friendship with him. And it was Berzins our thoughts turned to when we were discussing escape options.

In the course of grooming Berzins we became increasingly confident that he would cooperate, provided we could offer him some kind of quid pro quo. Now, whenever I had time alone with him I would talk about Scotland and my love of the country. I'd talk about Greece too and the Greek shipowners I'd worked for. I was introducing him to a world he'd only glimpsed. Berzins had transitioned straight from Soviet-era shipboard life to Soviet-era prison life. The world I spoke of was foreign to him and he liked the sound of it. Increasingly he would deluge me with questions, which I readily answered, lending a nostalgic view of my own experiences and how much I missed my old life. I didn't have to act the part.

Finally, and after further discussion with Valdis, I broached the subject. Finding the opportunity to speak privately with anyone, let alone a senior guard, was never straightforward, but Berzins liked to share sailors' stories with us and he'd often visit the laundry room when he knew we were working there.

On this day, a week after my meeting the Farrington, he wandered in banging his truncheon on top of the machines as he passed to add to the din they were already making. 'Why aren't you working, you lazy bastards?' he shouted in English. It was his standard greeting.

I dived in: 'Janis, we need to talk. Something important.'

'What, you want to get out of here? Tell me something I didn't know, eh?'

'Actually, that is it. We need your help to get us out of here. I mean, all three of us. In return we'll do everything we can to get you settled in the UK or any other EU country; start a new life – with some serious money in your pocket.

We can't guarantee it, but between us Valdis and I have influence. I'm expecting another visit from a senior British official with a lot more influence than us. When he comes you can make sure you're on duty in the visiting room and you'll see him. What do you think? He can help.'

It was a risky approach. I had no idea at this point when or who my visitor would be, but I was pretty sure it wouldn't be Dominic Farrington again.

I thought I'd overplayed my hand. He stared at me as if I'd suggested he should join us on a trip to a distant planet. 'What? What are you saying?'

'Janis, forget it. We just get frustrated in here. Neither Valdis nor I belong in this place and you know it. I just thought …'

'Okay, okay. I understand. Just let me think about it. It's very risky, but let me think.' He paused. 'How to do it? And how much?'

'We have a plan. And I'm sure something can be arranged that would satisfy you: money and help with visas, permits …' I had no idea whether the British government would see the benefit of paying off a Latvian prison guard to assist in a breakout, but desperate times demanded desperate measures, I told myself.

A week later I had a visitor. I hadn't expected the Admiral to visit personally. And when he did, I hadn't expected him to be wearing full dress uniform – gold braid, medals and all – but I was nonetheless surprised how ordinary he looked. Despite the warm weather he was wearing a grey overcoat under which was a grey suit. He was of average height. His hair was grey and thinning, and he wore glasses. He sat down behind the glass panel facing me. The light reflected off his glasses so I couldn't see his eyes behind them. He sat motionless and when he spoke his voice was low and without accent or emphasis. It was hard to imagine him commanding a squadron of Her Majesty's warships. It wasn't so difficult to imagine him running a network of spies though. He might have been George Smiley's brother.

'Humming Bird is here I gather. Perhaps you would like to tell me how you think I can help you,' he said. 'Is it he or you I am here for?'

I told him that mine was a case of justifiable homicide. I had acted in self defence and was therefore blameless and innocent. 'As for my fellow prisoner, I believe you know his case. You must understand that failing our prompt release from here we are committed to escape – do or die. And the guard standing behind you,' I added, 'is willing to assist in a breakout, under certain conditions.'

Berzins was a good six metres away on the other side of the room and showing no sign of listening but I still spoke softly, leaning forward as I did.

'Well, it's very obliging of you to share your thoughts,' the Admiral replied caustically. 'They are nothing if not ambitious. I've already been looking at your case. But tell me about our friend? Is he well?'

'No, he's not.' I told him about the shower incident and how it had shaken him up. 'I presume you want him out of here in one piece as much as he does. He has critical information to share.'

'About what, precisely?'

'Loose nukes.'

'What about them?'

'One warhead has been stolen from the Zeltini missile base. Our friend knows who took it and believes he can help track it down before it gets launched in anger. There may be others disappearing from Zeltini as we speak.'

'I see. So who's behind this?'

'He says a rogue GRU gang.'

'Any idea what kind of missiles we're talking about?'

'OTR-21 Tochka with a nuclear warhead. He said you'd understand.

'Yes, short range ballistic missile, the SS-21 Scarab. It could wipe out a small city. Transported in a 9P129 vehicle.

The missile is raised prior to launch. Presumably that was part of the consignment too?'

'He mentioned the transporter, yes. Oh, and he has the launch code. It seems those who stole the missile omitted to take the code. He said this would be useful too, to keep it out of their hands.'

'Humming Bird has it? How the hell did he get hold of that?'

'He stole it. He said he'll give you more information once he's out.'

'You mean he doesn't trust us. I can't say I blame him. He must have lost faith in us, but you can assure him we've used all means to locate him. The last place we expected him to turn up was here. I'm presuming you know something of our friend's background?'

'Yes.'

'Alright. Tell him this: we will pull him out as quickly and safely as we can. To be blunt, he's a liability in here. If those GRU brutes, whether rogue or not, choose to interrogate him in earnest, he could give them an awful lot of information we would rather keep to ourselves. And now this missile business makes it doubly urgent. I'd rather have kept him in place where he was, as a Ventspils harbourmaster, but that's out of the question now they've got him locked away in here. Any idea what he wants?

Country cottage with roses and wisteria in the garden? That sort of thing?'

'We haven't got that far, but he's concerned about his daughter in Vienna.'

'Yes, we have her on file. I need to be in Vienna shortly to talk to the IAEA about this whole business – the maritime dimension of missiles going astray. It's a potential nightmare. Anything else?'

'Yes. Our friend standing behind you will need looking after too.'

'Money?'

'And a ticket out, visa – facilitation. He'll be in danger too if he remains in this country.'

'Where does he want to go?'

'Greece.'

The Admiral leaned back in his chair. 'I see. So, three of you. Well let's see what can be done. I'll be raising this to a high priority exfil. When your plans are finalised, ask to see the consul again. Next time it'll be one of my people, and it'll be quick. Give him a time and a date and where you all want to be met. We'll take it from there. Can you manage that?'

'I'm sure we can,' I said, trying to sound confident. 'He and I share the same purpose. And he's a good man. He doesn't deserve to end his days in this place.'

'Yes, I agree.'

He got up and gestured to Berzins to unlock the door.

Chapter 14

Daugavpils, Latvia

June 1999

Starting a prison riot, let alone controlling one, is not a simple task, but given the conditions in White Swan, it was a tinderbox of violence waiting to be ignited anyway. Overcrowding, understaffing, the brutal caste system – all contributed, but the spark that ignited it came from Berzins. The caste system imposed and sustained by the prisoners themselves had become an institution in itself. So the changes Berzins started introducing, aimed at destabilising the fragile status quo, quickly became deeply unpopular.

It began with the haircuts: shaved heads all round. Then came a strictly enforced smoking ban, and most contentious of all, a mixing of the three castes at meal times. Old rules that had been ignored for years were suddenly enforced and accompanied by random and savage beatings administered with truncheons by Berzins and his men. What made it worse was that these measures were only applied in G Block. And Berzins' junior colleagues had no choice but to follow his lead as he was only following long-established prison rules, never mind that they hadn't been obeyed for as long as anyone could remember. But quite deliberately now, enforcement of the rules was inconsistent and arbitrary.

Prisoners began complaining about putrid food too. Berzins had been in the kitchens telling the cooks to serve food that was on the verge of going rotten in order to avoid wastage.

His justification was simple. He had been ordered to break the caste system. Bringing it down had been a standing order for years, but no one had had the balls to try. When Berzins stepped forward offering to do it, his superiors consented because they knew it simply meant complying with the rules. They could hardly object. What they didn't realise was the abruptness and severity with which it would be carried out. Other blocks would follow but G Block was where it would start. Over the next two weeks the pressure built. How long can this go on, Valdis would ask. Other prisoners, VIPs particularly, would ask the same question. You could feel the tension: the look on their faces, their body language, their furtive conversations. A sense of foreboding took hold.

'I can't say for sure, but it's imminent.' I told the Admiral's man when he visited. 'Can you have your people standing by starting tomorrow, every day?'

'I'll see what I can do.'

'That's not good enough,' I said. 'I need your assurance. The situation is highly volatile.'

'I can see that. Don't worry. We'll be ready.'

'So from tomorrow 0600 hours, or is that a bit too early for you?'

'Alright then,' he sighed, ignoring my sarcasm. 'There's a track across the road from the west wall. We'll be in the trees there, watching 24/7 from 0600. Does that work for you?'

'Yes. What sort of transport? So we can recognise you?'

'It'll be a Lada.'

'Colour?'

'Grey.'

Three days later a group of prisoners rushed into G Block's dining hall and barricaded themselves inside just after ten in the morning. It was a rampage. They destroyed furniture and smashed anything else they could lay their hands on. Tables and chairs flew. The two attendants in charge of clearing up after breakfast escaped back into the kitchen but the prisoners followed, taking them both hostage.

Then inmates from other blocks surged past guards and into the central exercise yard. A tower guard fired a shot at a prisoner trying to climb over an internal fence. The man fell to the ground and lay still. This triggered an uproar. As the situation escalated, fires were started, guards were beaten and after a few hours it was clear that the inmates had taken control of the whole prison. Word spread that sixteen were dead, both guards and prisoners, and many others injured. At around four in the afternoon a couple of police helicopters were seen hovering overhead. But they were only there to survey the situation and soon flew off. At six that evening a detachment of heavily armed police arrived to restore order which, over several more hours of violence and chaos, they succeeded in doing. The insurrection had been quelled. For now. But the atmosphere was tense and febrile.

Throughout the day we saw no sign of our GRU friends, which made me uneasy. But it was time for us to go, Berzins included. He had supplied us both with guards' uniforms, which we struggled into. Our escape route was through G Block's laundry room, where we'd spent so much time on work duty and knew the layout back to front. On one side of the long room were lines of old washing machines, half of which were either worn out, had been smashed up, or were otherwise out of use. On the other side were the laundry carts, where sheets and clothing were dumped. At the far end was a large steel door covered in flaking orange paint. This led out to a yard into which the trucks would reverse to deliver the clean and pick up the dirty laundry. This was from years ago, before the machines had been installed. These days the door was never used, until now.

We stood outside the laundry room awaiting Berzins' signal telling us the coast was clear, which came after less than a minute: a short, barked command. We entered and hurried to where he was waiting by the orange door. An attending guard lay slumped in a heap beside him. Berzins returned his truncheon into its belt loop, removed a ring of keys from the unconscious guard's own belt and unlocked the heavy door.

Outside it was raining heavily. We moved quickly up across a yard towards the gate that led out of the prison. There were watchtowers either side of this external gate, each within firing range. The whole scene was lit by powerful search lights. Puddles of water bounced a shimmering light off the ground. Sirens were wailing and uniformed guards and police were running in all directions. The suppression of the riot hadn't lasted.

Berzins' acting was masterful as he seemingly took command of the situation, shouting and pointing with his truncheon while gradually moving us towards the gate. Now he was shouting at the guards, but they were looking doubtful, uncertain whether to obey or challenge. It was turning into a confrontation. Valdis and I held back, but there were guards advancing now to join the row as it began to escalate beyond a shouting match. The gate guards were holding their ground despite Berzin's commands. Then without warning came a blinding flash and the boom of explosives. The steel gate was suddenly collapsing inwards and on the far side were men in black clothing, body armour, helmets and masks, each armed with an assault rifle. For a moment, everyone stood frozen in the harsh light, like figures caught in a camera's flash.

'Go!' I yelled, grabbing Valdis by the arm, Berzins following. I assumed that since they'd blown in the door from the outside, the men in black were there to help free us. Now I doubted it. Their focus seemed to be on the rioting, and in the chaos they ignored us as we clambered over the wreckage of the steel gate. We sprinted across the road and found a track leading into scrubby woodland. Headlights flashed: the Lada.

Chapter 15

Daugavpils, Latvia

7 June 1999

I should have been shouting for joy, punching the air and drinking brandy from the hip flask the driver was passing round. Or better still, wandering among the pine trees that surrounded us, breathing in the heavy scent of resin and of freedom. But it wasn't like that. The three of us piled into the Lada. It turned and headed down the heavily rutted track into the woods; headlights off, the driver guided by instinct rather than sight. We were escaping, but it was too soon for celebrations.

Valdis, Berzins and the driver were talking intensely among themselves. It seemed we were travelling in the direction of the river, from where we would rendezvous with a boat and head downstream to Riga. But that's not what happened. We hadn't travelled more than a couple of miles when the driver braked suddenly. I leaned forward to see what the problem was. Parked across the track was a black van. Our driver veered off, trying to find a way round, but they'd chosen the site of their ambush carefully. Neither could we turn round, at least not in the time available, which was no more than thirty seconds before they were upon us:

Aramis, Athos and Porthos, the GRU hoods from White Swan.

We were dragged out of the car. Weapons were drawn, orders shouted and before any of us could react, Berzins and our driver were pulled aside to the edge of the forest. They were protesting at first, then when they realised what was happening, they turned to run and seek cover among the trees. I'd have done the same. Better to die trying to escape than meekly surrender to your fate. The clatter of automatic rifle fire seemed to go on for a long time as Aramis made sure neither of them got away. He walked over to examine his handiwork then returned, grinning, to where we were held, pinned against the van with pistols against our heads.

'See what will happen,' gloated Porthos, 'if you don't do what we tell you?'

We were bundled into the back of the van, Athos and Porthos either side of us, Aramis at the wheel. As we took off, Valdis said something to Athos in Russian. He got an elbow in the face and a single word of warning for his trouble. Athos was the quieter of the three but I sensed he was the most dangerous. He watched carefully and listened closely. Was he or Aramis the de facto leader of the three, I wondered.

The journey took over an hour. Every time I tried talking to Valdis I had a gun rammed into my ear and was told to shut up. They knew enough English anyway to understand if we were talking of escape or resistance, so I stayed silent.

They took us to what in the dark looked like an abandoned warehouse. Any sense of direction I might have had was lost, but I could see we were in some kind of run-down industrial zone on the outskirts of a town. Inside the dimly lit building as we were marched in, I could see high, empty storage racks divided by aisles. We were pushed and prodded down the centre aisle. The concrete floor was smooth and oily in patches. Forklifts or other cargo handling equipment had been in use here. At the far end directly ahead of us was an upright wooden chair. A man was tied to it, his head lolling down onto his chest.

'Your friend, English,' announced another man, who was walking towards us: average height and thin, thirtyish, so younger than the triplets. Black hair and hunched shoulders. He was wearing a long black leather coat that completed his crow-like appearance. I imagined he might have flapped down from a nearby tree. He certainly didn't fit the D'Artagnan role.

As we approached, the man tied to the chair lifted his head wearily. His face was swollen and covered in blood but he wasn't difficult to recognise. Dominic Farrington took one look at us before letting his head roll back onto his chest.

'He sang like a little bird,' said the crow. 'He told me all about your clever escape plans, where you would be met and where you would be taken.' His voice had a soft, modulated tone to the point of sounding effete. 'So my job could not have been made easier. However, he has, as you would say, outlived his usefulness, so if you would oblige, Kazimir?'

Kazimir, or Aramis as we knew him, stepped forward and without hesitating, loosed off a volley from the same automatic rifle he'd used on Berzins and the driver. Still tied to the chair, Farrington flew backwards, propelled by the force of the rounds, and struck the back wall. He lay still, a dark pool of blood spreading out across the concrete floor.

'Ozols will be familiar with our methods, but they may come as a surprise to you, English,' the crow continued. 'They are both direct and effective though. Your friend over there told us some but not all of your travel arrangements. He claimed he was not a spy, just a consular officer. However, it was enough. You won't be needing tickets or passports from him for any onward journey.'

He appeared unarmed. He may have had a gun on him but perhaps he considered it beneath him to wave it around. That would be for his henchmen. He was showing off his English for my benefit and for a moment I found myself wondering where he'd picked up this bizarre Bond villain façade. Only this wasn't a film set, and if nothing or no one intervened soon, we would be going the same way as poor Farrington. Crow was talking directly to Valdis in Russian now. I glanced around. The triplets were standing behind us, their weapons casually trained in our direction. Should I wait and see if Valdis could influence events in some way? I couldn't see how though.

The crow was standing a few yards in front of me, slightly to my left. Valdis was on my right and the triplets behind us. We were grouped at the end of the aisle, close to the brick wall where Farrington lay. As long as he was talking and didn't give them direct orders, I figured the triplets would hesitate before shooting. And he seemed to like talking. I stepped forward, hands spread and without rushing. 'Listen, I've got something important to tell you,' I said, smiling, arms wide and unthreatening. I didn't, other than that I was planning to kill him, but I needed to distract him. The good news, I kept telling myself, was that he didn't seem to be armed, or if he was he was too busy talking to bother drawing a gun. More likely, he trusted his henchmen to protect him. I'd seen that there was a patch of oil on the floor between us. As I drew closer, I moved to his left to avoid alarming him head-on, still acting as if I just wanted to talk. Then, feigning a slip on the oily floor, threw myself forward in a crouching position. More by accident than design my shoulder made contact with his gut. It didn't wind him but gave me a second or two to get behind, grabbing him clumsily in an improvised headlock, my right arm round his throat, my left forearm pressing into the back of his neck, compressing it front and back.

'Valdis! Get behind me!' I yelled.

He did and now he was pressed against the wall with me shielding him and the crow in front shielding me. I was strengthening my grip on him now. His feet had lifted off the ground and he was trying to talk while clawing at my arm to get it away from his throat while kicking at me with his feet, neither having much effect. I tightened my grip more and he began to choke.

The three goons had moved forward in unison but it was clear from their expressions and hesitant movements that they were not sure what to do next.

'Drop the guns – all of them, now! Or your boss dies,' I shouted, hoping that he was their boss and that the prospect of his imminent death was something that would worry them.

'Tell them!' I growled into the crow's ear, loosening my grip slightly so he could speak.

He croaked something to them before I tightened my grip again. He was still kicking feebly at my legs and now began making gurgling noises.

'Do it!' I shouted and Aramis, who had blown Farrington away minutes earlier, slowly laid his gun on the floor. The other two followed.

'Valdis, get the guns. Unload one, give me one and keep one for yourself.'

Keeping hold of the crow with my right arm still round his neck I took one of the AK-47s Valdis had gathered up.

I had the idea that using the crow as a shield and having disarmed the triplets, we could move back up to the entrance and escape in the van with the crow as a hostage. The three of us began by moving awkwardly round the goons, then backwards up the length of the warehouse aisle. Holding onto the crow while dragging him on the slippery floor was proving hard. The triplets were advancing towards us, unarmed but unencumbered. I was about to voice my concern to Valdis when he stepped out from behind me and raised Porthos' rifle. Perhaps they'd thought that we were sportsmen, that we'd play by a set of rules instilled in us through the British sense of fair play. But they'd misjudged Valdis. He was, after all, a trained agent and he knew the importance of quick affirmative action. Without hesitating he sprayed the three men with a hail of fire. It was a massacre: no screams, just the gunfire echoing round the warehouse, men collapsing and blood everywhere, spattered up the walls, gathering in dark pools across the floor.

‘Christ, Valdis,’ I yelled, staring at him in shock.

‘What?’ he retorted angrily. ‘You want me to leave them alive? What then? We’re never free of them? Is that what I should have done? They deserved it. And they would have killed us. This one said so.’ He pointed the barrel at the crow.

‘Okay. Let’s just get out of here.’ It wasn’t the time to start debating the rights and wrongs with him. I thought of Berzins. Valdis had told me he’d planned to cross the border into Poland where he had family, before heading for Greece. He would have had enough to get started in a new life there, or maybe he’d go back to sea. He’d have been safer there. All too late now.

In the shock and chaos of those moments I’d overlooked the threat from the crow, who I still had round the neck. But I’d loosened my grip and I’d not thought to check his pockets. I’d just assumed he was unarmed. But he wasn’t. And now from inside his pocket he fired at Valdis. The shot went wide as I jerked him back into my hold then grabbed at the pistol which was still in his hand inside his coat pocket.

‘Let him go and stand back,’ called Valdis.

‘No, not another. We may need him.’

‘We don’t need him. He’s a crook like others. Worse. Now get out of the way.’

As he spoke he moved towards us. I backed away, still holding onto the crow. But he was struggling, and we were on an oily patch of the floor. In trying to push back with his feet he lost his footing. He slipped down, out of my grasp and onto the floor, and as I moved back away from him, I slipped too. The crow probably had a couple of narrow choices. He could have tried to get behind me for cover or he could have lunged at Valdis. Instead, he scrambled to his feet and ran towards the warehouse door. Valdis fired a single shot and the crow went sprawling across the floor, crashing into the side of one of the metal storage racks. Then he lay still. We walked over to him. Valdis turned him over with his foot. Now he reminded me even more of a crow – a dead one.

The keys of the van were in the ignition. I took the wheel. 'We need to find our way back to the river,' I said. 'See if we can locate the rendezvous point.'

'Carry on, I will direct you.'

'Do you know where the rendezvous is?'

'The driver told me. We will find, don't worry.'

We drove in silence for a while. Finally, Valdis spoke: 'I am sorry if that shocked you, Angus. It was necessary.'

I was shocked, as much by Valdis's ruthlessness as by the killings themselves.

'They got what they deserved,' I said. 'And Farrington had told them too much about our plans. They had to be silenced.'

'You know, the boss was too busy trying to impress you,' Valdis mused. 'He got careless.'

'Been watching too many movies where the villain has to explain everything for the benefit of the audience.'

He laughed grimly and we drove on in search of the river.

Chapter 16

River Daugava, Latvia

7-8 June 1999

'Where is it then, Valdis?' Finding that river took forever, but the sense of hope hadn't deserted us, despite the shock of what had just happened and the exhaustion we both felt. The Daugava was further than we'd thought, and the search was made harder by the maze of byroads we were forced to navigate in the dark. Eventually we found ourselves heading northwards on a narrow road running alongside it. The river rises in the Valdai Hills midway between St Petersburg and Moscow, Valdis informed me, from where it flows on through Belarus into Latvia and eventually into the Gulf of Riga, making it one of Europe's longest rivers.

'Valdai Hills? Is that where your name comes from?'

He threw me a derisive look. 'My name derives from Latvian word for "rule", not from some Russian hill in middle of nowhere.'

'You really don't like them, do you.'

'The Russians? I have known and liked many Russian men and women over many years. I judge people as I find them. But the system? Soviet system? No, that I hate. Now, that system has gone. We will have to see whether new "system" is better or worse for Russia. I am not optimistic, but Latvia is an independent state now.'

We drove on into the night. I was about to ask him whether he knew where we were going when he said, 'You know what this means, don't you?'

'What?'

'This we are doing – for me, not you. You are escaping back to your own country. Me, I am being exfiltrated; drawn away from my own country. And I do not believe I will ever return.'

'Do you regret that?'

'Of course I do. But do I regret betraying Soviet system, apparatus? No, never. I was a fighter in the Cold War and I knew in my heart and my mind who was right and who was wrong. It was clear to me, even before Cuba.'

'If you don't stay here, where will you settle? Vienna, with your daughter?'

'No. Would not be safe.'

'Then would she be safe there?'

'This is one of things that worries me. One of many things. And now we are free I worry more. Am I really free? Where shall I settle? Where will she? I must talk with Admiral about it all.'

Every time we reached a junction where a bridge bisected the river, we would stop to identify where we were.

And every time we came to a riverside mooring, we would stop to check whether our boat was there, waiting.

'Cannot be much further,' Valdis kept saying. Now that we could sense freedom and he'd begun to worry about the future, he'd become desperate to contact his daughter, but we hadn't passed any phone boxes.

It was past midnight by the time we pulled up beside a derelict-looking wharf clinging onto the riverbank. Two men were standing beside a workboat with the words: Ships Agent, Crew and Stores on the cabin's side in English. We got out of the van and the shorter of the two men, who I could see now was the Admiral, stepped forward and greeted Valdis with a formal handshake, but I could see he could barely contain his delight. 'You made it! Well done!' He turned to me. 'And Angus too!' He punched me on the arm. 'What the devil happened ? We've been here hours. And your man Berzins? The driver? Where are they?'

I let Valdis tell him what had happened. They knew each other well despite their rare face-to-face encounters and now they were together, the Admiral had lightened up and I could see that the relationship between a double agent and his case handler was special – beyond mere colleagues or friends, they were comrades in arms. There was something intense and resolute about their exchanges. And the Admiral was a different man from the one who had visited me in White Swan.

We cast off and headed downriver. The water was calm and what current there was favoured us. The night was clear without much light pollution from the shore, so we could see the Milky Way clearly as a diagonal, luminescent swathe across the black canvas of the sky.

It took us another nine hours to reach the next rendezvous in our journey. For the first hour or so there was much lively conversation, mostly between Valdis and the Admiral. Then they fell silent and both Valdis and I dozed off in the cabin, drained by the gruelling events of the day, the drone of the engine and the boat's gentle motion on the water.

I woke with a start as we were approaching Riga's river port. The sun was rising and ships alongside already working, most of them loading timber or discharging containers. I recognised the berth where the *Electra M* had moored ten weeks earlier. There was more traffic on the river now: workboats like ours belonging to local agents, chandlers and stevedores, all competing with tugs and barges for room. The Admiral appeared with coffee. He handed me a mug and gently shook Valdis awake.

'All okay?' I asked him.

'All okay. We'll be passing the Mangalsala Pier within the next half-hour, then through the breakwater and out into the Gulf. From there it's another three or four hours, depending on the sea state. There'll be a bit of a swell but it shouldn't slow us up.'

Earlier Valdis had tried repeatedly to contact his daughter on the Admiral's Nokia. Now he was trying again. I sought to reassure him. 'Maybe she switches it off at night.'

'Never.'

'Well then, the battery's flat. And doesn't she have a landline?'

'You don't understand. She is very organised. Would not let it go flat. She doesn't know where I am. She will be worried about me. And no, she does not have landline yet. She has applied for one. It takes time.'

'Let's wait until we get to our destination shall we?' suggested the Admiral. 'I can assure you, our people in Vienna will have been in touch with her and she'll be fine.'

He had told him this once already and Valdis, having slept, seemed to accept it – for now at least.

'Why all this way by boat?' I asked. 'Road would have been quicker.'

'And riskier. We're pretty inconspicuous on the water. And we don't have to change transport. We'll do that from Ruhnu.'

'Where is Ruhnu? Is there an airfield there?'

'Yes. It's an Estonian island out in the Gulf. I wanted to get us out of Latvia. Ruhnu's a safe place to make the transfer. From there it'll be a long flight back.'

'Where are we heading?'

'Scotland, old boy. Where else?'

We reached the island shortly after nine in the morning. The coxswain tied the boat up to a pontoon just beyond the ferry berth and we stepped ashore to be met by a large, bearded individual who introduced himself as Sven. 'I'm your pilot,' he announced. 'I'm from Sweden.'

Sven had thoughtfully brought along a cooler box containing sandwiches stuffed with cheese, ham, caviar, tomatoes, cucumber and accompanied by a spread he called *messmör*.

'It's Norwegian,' he said, 'but don't let that put you off.'

It didn't. It was the best food I'd tasted since leaving the *Electra M*. We'd landed on the southern tip of the island and Sven had parked his plane nearby at that end of the airstrip. So it was only a fifteen minute walk from the pontoon where we'd landed. We were in Estonia and I was relieved to be out of Latvian jurisdiction. I allowed myself to relax a bit. Now I could smell the pine resin. Was this the beginning of the end of the ordeal? Would the Admiral shield us from further risks? I looked at Valdis. He was visibly calmer. That fifteen minutes was the furthest either of us had walked since our incarceration.

Sven took the little plane up steeply over the heavily wooded island before making a left turn west and out into the Baltic. Surely now we'd left the dead hand of the GRU behind us. As if reading my thoughts I heard Valdis saying to the Admiral: 'Thank you, my friend. Now we are safe.'

The Pilatus Porter's range was more than enough to reach the Scottish coast and as I looked out of the window at the choppy waters below I thought of my last visit there many years before. I'd lived with my uncle and aunt in Leith from the age of eight after my parents and sister had been killed in a landslide in Hong Kong, where my father was a marine police officer. Scotland had been my home for ten years or so before I'd gone to sea. My uncle and aunt were both dead now, so I'd had little reason to go back.

'Why Scotland?' I asked the Admiral, who was sitting next to me.

He looked forward to the cockpit but Sven was preoccupied with flying the plane and couldn't hear us anyway above the noise of the engine.

'It's the nearest point in the UK to where we're coming from. So I've arranged a meeting there to take stock – discuss the way forward.'

At a cruising speed of just 230 knots, the flight seemed to go on for ever. The seats were uncomfortable too, though that didn't stop us sleeping.

But I woke suddenly, my heart thumping as my mind tried to make sense of what was happening. The plane was both rolling and diving at once. I could see lights flashing and hear alarms buzzing in the cockpit. Sven was shouting and from outside came the clearly audible scream of a jet engine. I stared out of the window to see a plane above us, red star markings clear on its wings and tail.

'Fockin' MiGs! Foxhounds!' yelled Sven. 'They're buzzing us. We're getting wake vortex off them! Check seatbelts and hold on!'

The plane continued to dive, levelling out just above the waves. From the window I could see oil rigs off to my left.

'How many MiGs?' the Admiral called.

'Two.'

'Are they attacking?'

'You could say that!' yelled Sven.

'I mean are they trying to bring us down?'

'Dunno, but they'll have a job now. No way can they fly this low.'

'Where are we?'

'Hundred and fifty miles west of the Danish coast.'

'We need to contact RAF Lossiemouth,' called the Admiral. 'Get some Tornadoes out here.'

I struggled forward to speak with Sven myself. 'RAF Lossiemouth? Can we contact them?'

He had steadied the aircraft but the MiGs were still visible above us. I could see one of the pilots clearly. He wasn't giving us a friendly wave either.

'Already on their way. Look.' He pointed to a screen. 'This is data relayed from ground radar. It's coming from Lossiemouth. Shows four aircraft approaching. Fast!'

I crouched behind him, staring at the screen as the aircraft moved closer. Then I looked up as the MiG on our starboard side suddenly banked and veered off and away. From where we were, it was all over in less than a minute, as if it had never happened.

Sven was sweating. 'Jesus! I've heard of Quick Reaction Alert but that was something.'

'Did you see the RAF planes?'

'They're still with us, Tornados. Four of them, above and either side. Look.'

Kneeling and craning my neck, I peered up out of the cockpit windscreen. Valdis and the Admiral had no such view from their seats, obstructed by the high wing of the Porter, but from here I could see the sky above us and two of the Tornados. Sven was busy talking to them over the radio. When he stopped I tapped his shoulder.

'And the MiGs?'

'Gone. Both of them. And we'll never know whether they were trying to bring us down, turn us back or just scare the shit out of us.'

I moved back to update Valdis and the Admiral.

'Our GRU friends,' said the Admiral, 'rogue or otherwise, would seem to have some clout even up here.'

'Bastards!' said Valdis with feeling.

Chapter 17

North Berwick, Scotland

8-9 June 1999

We landed at East Fortune, once home to a First and then a Second World War airfield that had since been transformed into a flight museum. Neither of us had passports, and having gone through a perfunctory customs and immigration check in an old and damp concrete hut some way off the runway, we walked out past a decommissioned delta wing RAF bomber parked on the apron outside a hangar. It reminded me of the giant manta rays we used to see breaching off the Mexican coast.

'One of two surviving Vulcans to have engaged the enemy in those hair-raising Black Buck missions,' the Admiral announced. 'They flew them down to Ascension, then on to the Falklands with in-air refuelling along the way. Bombed Port Stanley airfield, but to be honest those raids weren't terribly effective. And this particular old bird caused an international incident when it had to divert to Brazil. You can see both mission markings and a Brazilian flag painted on the nose.'

'Why weren't they effective?' I asked.

'Because they weren't intended for that kind of work. They were part of the V-force, the backbone of our airborne nuclear deterrent during the Cold War. And for the most part they were armed with nuclear weapons. Theirs was more of a high-altitude strategic role to patrol over Europe. Bet you didn't know that, did you, Valdis.'

'Of course I knew,' he said winking at me. 'It was our job to know everything you were doing.'

'Humbug!' the Admiral grunted. 'I bet you didn't know that you could roll those beasts either.'

'Impossible!'

'No. One was famously rolled back in 1955 by Avro's chief test pilot. His name was "Rolly" Falk. He received a sound bollocking of course from the Avro directors but they were secretly delighted.' We all laughed. Anything unrelated to the events we'd just left behind brought on a sense of elation.

From the airfield we were taken in a black unmarked Ford eastwards along the backroads of East Lothian until we reached the coast.

'Welcome to Gin Head,' declared the Admiral with satisfaction and a note of relief at having finally brought us to our destination in one piece. 'You've never heard of this place and you'd be well advised to forget you were ever here. It was used as an early warning station to alert the RAF to incoming enemy aircraft. Not any more though.'

On the face of it, it was just a long-abandoned collection of grey, nondescript concrete huts, albeit on a spectacular clifftop site overlooking the North Sea. But I didn't want to spoil things for the Admiral, whose guided tour would have been a credit to any estate agent.

'This place allowed the RAF to scramble fighters to the exact areas under attack; that's why the RAF always appeared to be in the right place at the right time. The Luftwaffe never recognised its importance. And the "Window" technique was developed here too: dropping bundles of aluminium from an aircraft which would deflect enemy radar signals and jam their stations. Owned by BAE nowadays but we still have our own safe house here.'

'So it was used in the Cold War?' Valdis asked.

'Ah, well. That's "need to know", old chap. But put it this way, you're not the first guest from the Eastern Bloc to pass through these doors.'

By this point he'd taken us down steps into what looked like an underground bunker but once inside, turned out to be a modern, well-furnished apartment with a lounge, dining room, kitchen and three ensuite bedrooms, all of which faced east onto the North Sea. Items of neatly folded clothing were laid out in two of the bedrooms, their labels still attached and a pair of scissors provided to remove them.

An attractive, petite blonde in her early thirties stepped into the room. She was wearing a white lab coat, unbuttoned the way doctors do when wanting to appear professional and busy, but casual at the same time.

'Ah, Doctor, come and meet our guests,' effused the Admiral. 'Gentlemen, this is Dr Kirstin Mackenzie. And she wants to give you each a thorough examination. Also, she's very kindly been shopping for you.'

'I hope the clothes fit,' she said. 'I was up in Edinburgh for ages yesterday. Not used to buying for men, and the Admiral was very approximate in his description of you both. I'd like to have a look at Mr Ozols first if I may – now. You look as if you'll live,' she added, addressing me.

We left Valdis in her care and went back into the living area.

'Valdis and I need to have a hush-hush session tomorrow, Angus. You should take yourself off somewhere. It's a beautiful coast and you've got North Berwick just down the road.'

'I could do with a break. I don't like being cooped up.'

'I can understand that.'

It was another hour before Valdis and the doctor emerged from the bedroom.

'Your turn,' she said in a brusque tone of voice.

When we were in the bedroom I asked her how Valdis was. 'Considering his age and what he's been through, pretty good. He's got a strong heart and he's not overweight, which helps enormously. Now, take your clothes off.'

'If you like.'

'Don't get cheeky. Just down to your underwear.'

After she'd finished she asked, 'How are you feeling – mentally I mean, in yourself?' I realised now why she'd taken so long with Valdis. She was as interested in how our minds had fared as much as our bodies.

'Fine. But I need to get out of here for a bit, breathe the air of freedom. Valdis has a private session with the Admiral tomorrow so I'll take myself off somewhere. I don't feel like I'm quite back to real life yet.'

'I see. Well, maybe I can arrange something.'

'I'd appreciate that.'

'How about I pick you up at ten tomorrow morning?'

That evening the Admiral insisted on updating us with what had been going on in the world while we'd been incarcerated: in particular, developments in the Balkans, where Serbia was now at war with Kosovo, and Yeltsin's firing of his prime minister, Yevgeny Primakov, in the latest convulsion of his presidency. Within minutes Valdis was slumped in his wing chair, snoring loudly.

Having slept like the dead myself, I awoke to the sound of gulls screeching outside my bedroom window as they performed their aerial acrobatics against a clear pink and blue sky. It was a beautiful late spring morning and the sun, as it rose over the sea, streamed into the room. To my right was Tantallon Castle, the often besieged and now ruined fourteenth-century fortress of the earls of Angus. To my left was the Bass Rock, the gannets already swarming over the vertical cliff faces of the volcanic rock, up north from their overwintering in Africa.

I was free, and it felt good. And I could look forward to a day out with a beautiful woman. She picked me up in a little sports car and, with the hood down, we drove into North Berwick. I looked across at her as she drove, her hair blown wildly by the wind. She was smiling, aware of my attention.

She parked next to the Lodge, a meadow-like park sloping down to the town and the seafront. We ate fish and chips and walked along the beach, talking and laughing.

'My parents keep a house here. We'd always come down for our summer holidays. Now I get to use it if I'm working at Gin Head.'

'Is that often?'

No, maybe two or three times a year, but it can be for days or sometimes weeks at a stretch.'

'MoD?'

'Yes, and more than that I cannot say so don't be so nosy. Come on, I'll show you my wee place.'

It was an Edwardian terraced house right on the seafront. 'These places fetch the earth now but it was nothing special when my parents bought it. They've done a lot to it over the years though.'

It was crammed with an eclectic mix of furnishings, ornaments and art, much of it from far-off places and all tastefully arranged. It seemed a lot more than just a holiday home.

'How about a wee drink to celebrate your freedom?'

'Great idea. What have you got there?' She was pulling a bottle of champagne out of the fridge.

'Taittinger do? I've been saving it for a special occasion but I never expected to be entertaining a bosun! Are you married to the sea? What's your plan after you've done whatever it is you have to do?'

'Here, give me that,' I said, helpfully reaching for the bottle.

'What! Do you think I can't open a bottle of bubbly? God, you've been at sea a long time.' She skilfully eased the cork out and poured.

'I'm sorry,' I said, taking the glass from her. 'No, I'm not married to the sea. In fact, I'm not planning to go back.'

'So what are you planning?'

'Not sure. Maybe set up a little claims business in Greece. I know some shipowners in Piraeus.'

'Sounds boring.'

I laughed. I found I was laughing quite a lot in her company. 'How about you?'

'I didn't fancy life as a GP so I did an ACCS acute care programme: intensive care, anaesthetics, trauma and paediatrics – that kind of thing. That took me into the military and from there into more sensitive stuff with the MOD, like what I'm doing now. Oh, and I've been doing quite a few EMRS jobs, mostly off North Sea oil rigs and some of the isles and remote rural places.'

'What's EMRS?'

'Emergency Medical Retrieval Service - medevacs to you. That's about it in a nutshell.'

'I'm impressed. And you are the most beautiful doctor I've ever encountered.'

'Is that because all the others have been men?'

She was laughing again. I finished the glass, put it on the table and moved closer to her.

'You know, ever since I examined you I could tell what was on your mind.'

'Is that why you invited me here?'

'Maybe,' she said playfully. 'Shall we finish this upstairs then?'

Slowly, standing at the foot of the bed, she began taking off her clothes. First she undid her tight shirt, button by button, taking her time. Underneath she had on a skimpy black bra.

'Give me a hand,' she said and pulled me towards her. We kissed as I undid her bra and she began pulling my shirt undone.

'You know, I've never invited anyone back here. Never. And I'm not sure whether to feel guilty or just excited.'

We fell back onto the bed together.

Chapter 18

North Berwick – Leuchars RAF base, Scotland

10-11 June 1999

We stood at the lounge window looking out across the North Sea. Four large tankers were anchored a few miles offshore. 'Waiting for orders,' the Admiral stated. 'They load North Sea crude at BP's Hound Point terminal up by the bridges.'

'Interesting,' I said. He was a mine of information and enjoyed sharing it. 'But I'd like to know what happens next. It's hardly begun, has it?'

'No, it hasn't, but we have good news. We've made contact with Valdis's daughter. They've spoken at some length. She's in Vienna. And as we expected, she is well. She'll be meeting us when we get there.'

'That's where we're going, is it? Was there a problem?' I wondered if this was more of a family reunion than an assignment.

'She just didn't know what had happened to him. How could she? We tracked her down via one of our embassy people, who visited her apartment. The old man was much relieved to hear from her. And there's another reason, which we'll get to when he joins us. But I need to put something to you first, Angus. You no doubt know far more than you should about our dealings with Valdis. And naturally, we shall be asking you to sign the Official Secrets Act at some point. However, you are under no obligation to continue your involvement in this matter. You are not a servant of the British government and we can release you from any commitments or responsibilities you may feel that you have. We can get you back to Greece or wherever it is you wish to go, and that will be that.'

'Listen,' I said. 'I met him in gaol. He told me his story at great length. I feel I know him better than anyone and we built a strong bond. We've been through hard times together. We're friends. I'm not going to walk away from him now. But I'll stay only if he wants me to stay.'

'Well, I'm glad to hear that. He expressed something similar to me.' He hesitated. 'You understand of course that by the very nature of things, I shall be in command.'

'I never had the slightest doubt,' I said, feeling a little apprehensive as to just what that might mean.

'Good. Oh, and new passports are on their way for you both. Now then, our friend revealed something yesterday that you need to hear. And as I say, he's also made it abundantly clear that if we are to pursue the case, as we must, then he wants you along too.'

He walked over to a house phone. 'Valdis, join us now, will you.' It wasn't a question. This was the Admiral displaying his military colours: ordering rather than asking.

No one could describe the Admiral as cool, or even current. Much of his language was a throwback to days gone by, but his decisive, authoritative manner commanded attention. Valdis came through and I poured more coffee.

'Tell him what you told me yesterday about your concerns.'

Valdis sat down and turned to me. He looked weary.

'Are you alright?' I asked. 'You've spoken to Iveta, I hear.'

'Yes, and that is great relief. She has been very worried. And also she wants me to visit because she is performing a piano recital. She is nervous performing before many people and she wants me there. I must be there for her. Admiral said it is dangerous for me to be in Vienna but she is my daughter. I would go anyway.' He gave the Admiral a look.

'But listen, Angus, I did not want to trouble you with this my friend, but if we are to work together to trace final receiver of this weapon you must know everything that I know. I have shared it with Admiral and I must share with you now.

'You know I was worried about Iveta. Not just love of father for his daughter. It is through her work in IAEA, I worry. She is only intern you know, but she tell me when we last talk before prison that IAEA has special department for finding nuclear weapons that have been stolen. Incident and

Trafficking Department, it is called. She already worked in this department for two weeks as training and was very interested in what they do. And now she has boyfriend, Latvian man older than her. She meet him when she worked there. I told Admiral I am not so happy about my daughter knowing this man. He is from Latvia, but ethnic Russian. I did not want to get her involved in anything that might put her in difficult situation. I did not want her to know anything that I knew about missiles that were missing from Zeltini. Can be dangerous. Every nuclear device has built-in security mechanism: unlock and launch authorisation code. The Soviet missile codes were held by General Staff at command centres to be sent direct to weapons commanders. Weapons commanders could then execute launch procedures. As you know, I have the code for the Zeltini missile that went missing.'

'Tell me more about these codes,' I said. I didn't want to misunderstand what was clearly an area of common knowledge to the two of them.

The Admiral intervened. 'PAL – Permissive Action Link. It's an access control security device to prevent unauthorised arming or detonation of a nuclear weapon. For example, while Ukraine had physical control of the Soviet weapons on their territory, it didn't have operational control of them as they were dependent on Russian-controlled electronic Permissive Action Links and the Russian command and control system.'

'And Valdis, where do you have the code? In your memory?

'Yes, in memory, here,' he tapped his head. 'It is eight-digit code.'

'Is it wise for you to be going into enemy territory so to speak, with that in your head?' I preferred not to think what would happen if anyone tried to force it out of him. He was at risk in White Swan. Now he was stepping right back into harm's way. I expressed my concerns to them both.

'First, I cannot un-remember it, can I? Better it stays here in my head. Also, I cannot forget my responsibility. It is my duty to find it.'

'Is there any way this PAL code can be broken into or side-stepped?'

'Let me tell you,' the Admiral answered, 'bypassing a PAL is about as straightforward as performing a tonsillectomy while entering the patient from the wrong end.'

'Okay, so how could all this play out?'

'The boyfriend has been vetted,' said the Admiral, 'and he probably works hard and does a good job, but if it makes Valdis jumpy it makes me jumpy too. What if the boyfriend isn't quite who he seems? It's just too damn risky to have

Valdis go down to Vienna alone. I'd rather he didn't go at all but short of locking him up here, there's not much I can do to stop him. He's entitled to see his daughter perform. And at the end of the day, he's the best man for the job – of locating the missile I mean. It's high risk but he'll be supported, by you, me, and Six's Vienna station are there if we need them. We're going into this anticipating every possible outcome, every worst case scenario.'

'You're as paranoid as Valdis.'

'Yes, I am. And in our business, it pays to be. If you're not, you're a liability, to yourself and to others. Suppose something is revealed to the boyfriend by Iveta in passing – some reference by her father to shipments of military equipment from Zeltini through the port of Ventspils, for example, in his role as a harbourmaster there. A bottle of wine over dinner after a hard day's work, shop talk, office gossip, news of home in Latvia, family: careless talk, pillow talk … it happens. Something is said that can't be unsaid. And it gets passed on. They, the GRU illegals, know Valdis has escaped from prison. They may know his daughter lives and works in Vienna. They need the PAL code. They may guess Valdis will come to see his daughter. They suspect he has the code ...'

'All this is speculation. So many hypotheticals.'

'Yes, you're right. And that's what we deal in: "what-ifs". And if there is the slightest chance of such a scenario playing out, we act. That's why we're going to Vienna with Valdis, and we'll be on an operational footing. As things are, we're sitting on one hell of a security risk.'

'So you see now,' said a sombre Valdis. 'These are my fears.'

'Anything is possible, however unlikely it seems sitting here. We'll keep an eye on the boyfriend. Six have got a horde of people in Vienna. We'll have him followed, bug the flat, intercept his comms.'

Valdis looked worried: 'You mean her flat. That's where they live – together. Is it necessary?'

The Admiral shrugged.

'Talking of "what-ifs",' I said, 'there's another scenario.'

'What's that?'

'Iveta is onto the Russian "boyfriend" and is monitoring him on behalf of others. The IAEA, Austrian Intelligence, Latvian Intelligence? Are you sure she's not working for the British? MI6, some other agency?'

'Rest assured, I would know. But at least you're thinking like a spy now. Nothing can be ruled out. Under your premise she could even have been set up to act as a honey trap.'

'Please!' Valdis exclaimed.

'And in practical terms, what are we going to be doing, apart from attending a piano recital?'

'It's about being cautious, prudent. It's what we do in this game: cover all bases. But there's been further intel I haven't told you of which makes this all the more vital, came through last night. More chatter than hard fact, but interesting for us nonetheless. Ever heard of Gagra?'

'A port on the Black Sea coast?'

'That's right. Abkhazia: something of a frozen conflict zone. There has been a number of seizures of nuclear materials smuggled from or through Abkhazia or South Ossetia over the last few years, this much we know. Now we've heard of some suspicious overland traffic spotted moving into Gagra over the past few days.'

'You think could be our Zeltini Tochka?' Valdis asked. 'Has anything been shipped out from port of Gagra?'

'Not that we know of. Best guess is that *if* they are missiles, or a single missile, then they'll be bound for the East Med or Near East. Syria or Lebanon most likely. The intel came from what the Israelis have picked up. All very tentative at present and no suggestion they're from Latvia.

'So, we talk to Iveta, I will talk with the IAEA and with our good friends at Six's Vienna station. We assess and we act on what we have learned. Remember, we're not just looking for a nuclear weapon, we're looking for the people who took it, the people who have bought it and what they're planning to do with it.'

***

A helicopter picked us up the following morning: Valdis, the Admiral and myself. And Kirstin. I sat next to her and we held hands like a couple of school kids, until she started squeezing my thigh.

'Are you coming with us?' I asked.

'Unfortunately not.'

Until she said that, I didn't realise how much I'd been thinking of her, and wanting to spend more time with her. I put my hand over hers.

We flew north out over the far edge of the Firth of Forth, the Isle of May to our west and on to the Fife coast before landing at RAF Leuchars.

It was hard saying goodbye to Kirstin. We'd only just met, but a lot had happened, and not just in bed. She was an enigma: the serious professional one minute and the fun-loving flirt the next. Or maybe I'd just fallen behind when it came to the ways of women – I'd been a long time at sea, and White Swan hadn't helped.

'Will I see you again?' I asked her.

'I hope so, my love.'

'We will then.' I hugged her self-consciously and walked over to what I was told was a RAF BAe146 that was to take us to Austria and God knows where beyond that. As we began taxiing down the runway I could see her waving and blowing kisses.

Chapter 19

Vienna, Austria

11-12 June 1999

Spittelberg is crammed with old apartment blocks, hidden squares and small, interesting-looking restaurants and bars. The tourists are told it's historical, but shabby would be a more accurate description. Our hotel hid itself on a quiet side street, a short walk from the city centre and a quarter of a mile from the Volkstheater underground station. The area had once been home to the red light district, though there was no sign of that now, but it did have a lively atmosphere, its streets thronged with young and old alike.

The three of us headed out to the Kleines Café, for that was where Iveta had suggested we meet. We took a circuitous route involving the subway and a taxi ride north of our destination before backtracking on foot. It was summer and customers filled the outdoor tables in the cobbled square in which the café sat overlooking St Jerome's Franciscan church which, I had read, had been consecrated in 1611. Kleines Café on the other hand had only been there since 1970, although the building in which it nestled went back to the Middle Ages, when it had been a public bath house. Like with any old town, Vienna's buildings and its geography gave the place its context, and its charm.

Iveta had insisted on meeting well away from the IAEA's headquarters. She was, after all, likely to be disclosing sensitive information without going through any formal channels and bumping into colleagues would have made our meeting uncomfortable, at the least.

We found a table and I was about to go in and order drinks when she appeared. The meeting of father and daughter, after all that had happened since they had last met, was an emotional moment for them both with much hugging and tears. Valdis introduced us and I offered to go in search of a waiter but she summoned one without difficulty. He'd been busy at another table, but was quick to come across and serve us, his eyes locking onto Iveta as she ordered for us.

Since she was not only a nuclear physics student but also an accomplished pianist, I'd expected a bespectacled bluestocking, but whether Iveta's genes were Slavic or Nordic, the result was striking. She had a heart-shaped face with big, blue-grey eyes, a wide forehead, high cheekbones and a wide mouth, all in perfect proportion and framed by a head of lustrous dark brown hair. There was no obvious resemblance to her father, but I came to recognise certain familiar physical mannerisms and inflections in her speech, though her English was more precise than his.

Our food and drinks arrived, sandwiches and beers for us, fruit juice for her.

'So, your recital begins at seven tomorrow evening, yes?' Valdis had switched into English for the Admiral's and my benefit.

'Yes, Papa, but I don't think your friends are here to talk about the recital.'

'On the contrary, my dear,' interrupted the Admiral, turning on the charm. 'We are looking forward to it. What will you be playing?'

It's a Chopin programme, a selection of mazurkas and waltzes ending with Nocturne in E flat major.'

'How beautiful. And we wish you well. Don't be nervous. Imagine you are playing it for yourself, and for your father of course.'

She laughed. 'Thank you. And for dear Mother too. I agree the Nocturne is a beautiful piece, but you haven't heard me play it yet. And I'm sure Papa has been exaggerating my skills.' She placed an affectionate hand on her father's arm.

'Well, we are looking forward to it, nevertheless. But you're right, there are other matters to speak of. First though,' he added looking at the busy tables around us, 'can we be sure we are safe to discuss such sensitive a subject here?'

'I believe so. I took steps to ensure I was not followed here from my office and I presume you did the same.'

'We did, and outdoors like this among a crowd is not a bad place to talk discreetly. What news do you have?'

'You may know that the IAEA's Incident and Trafficking Database Department relies on intelligence reports from many different sources, but they do not have their own field agents or any of that kind of infrastructure. For example, they may receive reports from your MI6 or from the CIA, and from the Russians too. Then they analyse all incoming intelligence and consolidate it into a report, which is updated of course as further information is received.

'So, what have we learned? A few days ago we hear of heavt military equipment, possibly missiles on transporters, arriving in the Abkhazi port of Gagra on the Black Sea. As you know, this is a disputed territory in the Caucasus between Georgia and Russia. And you may already have seen this report. But now, just this morning, we hear a ship is loading cargo in Gagra which includes a heavy vehicle and equipment, destination unknown. Only one vehicle. But the ship is interesting. It is a small river-sea vessel which left the port of Constantza two days ago and arrived at Gagra last night. The ship's name is *Phoenix Saturn* and it trades up and down the Danube, and to Black Sea ports.'

The Admiral leaned in. 'Do you think it is loading this Gagra cargo for the Danube?'

'They cannot say for sure but yes, it is possible.'

'Do you mind me asking where you came by this information?'

'I would rather not say,' she replied without hesitation. 'Only that it is reliable and there are often such exchanges between colleagues in different departments of the IAEA. We are mostly a transparent organisation.'

'The Danube,' I said. 'Serbia? Belgrade?'

'Which, of course,' she added, 'has been the subject of NATO's bombing campaign these past weeks. You will know of course, our reports are shared with NATO and other allied agencies.'

She sat back and took another sip of her fruit juice as we absorbed this news.

'Why the devil didn't I know about this?' blurted the Admiral. 'We track ships all the time – by satellite, via Lloyd's Agents ...'

'Because you didn't know what to look for,' Iveta answered sympathetically. 'Remember, the IAEA is constantly monitoring these missing weapons – the loose nukes. Their intelligence led them to Abkhazia and from there to the Danube.'

'Yes, some of this we knew, of course,' said the Admiral, 'but good grief, as you say, NATO is bombing Serbia as we speak. What the hell are these maniacs thinking of doing with a weapon like this? Do you have any idea who's behind it? I mean, we know about the GRU illegals trading these things, but to the Serbs? And the Russians are supposed to be allied with the West in this conflict. Just imagine: a missile armed with a nuclear warhead on its way straight into a battlefield. What if NATO planes were to bomb this *Phoenix Saturn* in error, through some communication cock-up? It wouldn't be the first time.'

We continued speculating on this latest development before the Admiral decided he needed to make some calls. I accompanied him back to the hotel, leaving Valdis and his daughter to spend the afternoon and evening together.

'For God's sake do be careful,' he warned before we left them.

'Don't worry,' replied Iveta smoothly. 'I think Papa has some experience in evasion methods.'

***

The Admiral was frustrated. 'We have a problem,' he declared that evening. We'd returned to the hotel using another roundabout route and I'd left him to it. It seemed his efforts to raise awareness had not met with much success. We'd arranged to meet for dinner in a little restaurant near the hotel I'd spotted. I was already halfway through a bottle of the local Blauer Zweigelt by the time he joined me an hour later than arranged, having aborted his efforts to raise the alarm in Whitehall, Belgrade or anywhere else. 'I'm having difficulty finding anyone who sees the importance of this. Mike Jackson's about to sign a peace agreement with this chap Marjanovic, supposedly bringing the war in Kosovo to an end, so that's what's top priority at present for both the military boys and the diplomats. It seems any intervention from NATO is out, for now at least. It's one of those back-burner situations they've said they'll keep an eye on. I warned them they bloody well better.'

I poured him a glass of wine which he downed as if it was there only to quench his thirst.

'Right, here's how I believe we should play this. I'll stay here with Valdis. I need to be close to the NATO people here anyway, and to the Six station and the IAEA too. Me getting bogged down in the Balkans isn't going to help get the attention of the right people. Go to Belgrade and see if you can track down the whereabouts of the *Phoenix Saturn*. I'll activate the Lloyd's Agent there. I met him once at some conference here in Vienna a few years ago and I judge him to be a capable character. By the time you've found the ship, I'll have worked something out to stop these mad bastards. That's the best I can do for now. We'll just need to keep in close touch. This one will be fast-moving, Angus.'

I'd become a bystander, now I felt I had a role to play again. And back at the hotel the Admiral gave me two black cotton bags. Inside one was a .38 revolver, in the other, a dozen or so bullets. I remembered my uncle taking me up into the Lammermuir Hills as a teenager and showing me how to use a twelve-bore. Then he'd pulled a Smith & Wesson .38 out of a bag just like the one I was holding now. 'This was your father's,' he'd said. 'Standard issue to the Royal Hong Kong Police Force. I'll keep it for you.' It was loaded and we'd spent the afternoon on improvised target practice.

'Ever used one of these?' the Admiral asked.

'A long time ago.'

'Your father's, wasn't it?'

'Yes, how did you know?'

'We're not without our means.'

***

Iveta's performance of her Chopin piece the next evening was impressive. I sat next to Valdis with the Admiral on his other side. Tears rolled down Valdis's cheeks and at the end, as she took her bow, the audience in the concert hall erupted in applause.

'Bravo!' cried the Admiral amid the cheering and wolf-whistles.

We waited in the foyer, the plan being to take her out to dinner in a smart Italian restaurant across the street. Iveta's boyfriend was working late and had not attended. Knowing how uneasy her father felt about him, I wondered if this was a diplomatic absence. After a few minutes she appeared, still dressed in the simple, low-cut black evening gown in which she had performed, but carrying a hold-all she'd retrieved from her dressing room. Valdis hugged her, we congratulated her and members of the audience stared, smiled and made approving comments as they passed us on their way out. A tall, grey-haired man with a neat goatee approached, bowed and kissed her hand. 'An exquisite performance, Fräulein,' he said in English, and bowed again before moving on. Several young women queued for her autograph. Iveta complied, looking embarrassed as she scribbled her signature on their programmes.

We headed down the steps and out onto the street, waiting to cross to the restaurant. I either didn't notice or don't remember what make or model of black car pulled up at the kerb. The three men who stepped out were in evening dress. They moved smoothly, surrounding us, smiling, talking, congratulating Iveta. With hindsight they had looked incongruous, their jackets too tight over muscular arms and shoulders, their hair close-cropped. As one of them continued with the charade the other two moved behind Valdis, grabbed him by his arms and bundled him into the back of the car before he had time to react. Belatedly I lunged forward towards the back door as it was closing. The third man elbowed me out of the way. I grabbed him by the lapels but it was a wasted effort. He tore himself free and made it into the front of the car, by which time it was on the move. With a squeal from the tyres, it shot down the street as he slammed the door shut. The whole episode had taken no more than a minute.

Iveta stared at us, stupefied, rooted to the spot.

'Let's get away from here,' I said, taking her by the arm. There were too many people still spilling out of the concert hall. We moved round the corner into a side street.

Iveta was taking deep breaths, trying hard to compose herself. 'My car is here. We must go after them. Did either of you see the numberplate?'

'Part of it,' I said. 'BG, then a red coat of arms, then the number. Belgrade?'

'Yes, of course! We must go there now. We must find him.'

'That means finding the *Phoenix Saturn* then, if Belgrade's where they're taking him.'

'Right, here's what's going to happen,' said the Admiral reasserting himself. 'I will call the Lloyd's Agent, Aleksandar Nenadovic, now. Iveta, how long will it take you to drive there?'

'It's about seven hundred kilometres I think, so maybe seven or eight hours.'

'Go now, with Angus. I can be of more use here. I have Nenadovic's address. Can you find it?' He pulled a notebook out of his pocket.

'We'll find him,' I said scribbling down a note of the address and phone numbers.

'He will be our point of contact then. If you can't reach me on this,' he said, waving his Nokia, 'get word through Nenadovic. You'll find him resourceful. Descended from some warrior nobility, he told me.' For the Admiral this was clearly the ultimate accolade.

'Okay,' I said. 'So it looks like, not only do those bastards know that Valdis has the launch code, but they've been unable to get at it by other means.'

'You're probably right. Just because they're ex-GRU doesn't mean they can tap into classified military secrets whenever they feel like it.'

Iveta was getting agitated. We parted company, the Admiral hailing a taxi and Iveta and I heading for where she'd left her Golf. And from there into a war zone.

Chapter 20

Vienna - Belgrade, Serbia

12-13 June 1999

I had my new passport with me, but little else. I'd left the Admiral's gun in my room safe, not thinking I'd need it. Clearly I had much to learn. Iveta had to collect her passport, which meant stopping off at her apartment on our way out of the city. We pulled up outside an elegant old building in a tree-lined street on the south side of the city.

'I'll be five minutes,' she said. I waited in the car and she came out after fifteen, having changed her clothes and showing no sign of panic now, just a controlled sense of urgency. She'd even brought a flask of coffee along with some food and cold drinks in a cooler bag.

'Was your boyfriend home?' I asked clumsily.

'I told you, he's working late. Why, are you suspicious? I told Papa, you have nothing to worry about. He's the last person on earth who would get involved in this kind of thing. And he hates the GRU, the KGB and all those Soviet-era spies and apparatchiks.'

'I'm sorry. I needed to hear that.'

We drove through the night, Iveta for the first couple of hours, after which I took over. Now she sat still and silent, staring at the road ahead.

'How long have you known of your father's spying?'

This time she was less troubled by the directness of my question, although I had intruded on her thoughts. 'Ten years perhaps. I was in my mid-teens. He had become withdrawn. We were always close. He played such an important part in my life, in encouraging my interests in music, and in science too. Then came the end of the Soviet regime, and our Singing Revolution and independence. We were so happy. And one day he took me to a park in Riga. It was after a demonstration we had been in the capital for, just the two of us. We sat on a bench in the sunshine and he told me how he'd sat there on the same bench with an Englishman, his friend and handler who was retiring. At first I had no idea what he was talking about, but then it all came out: Cuba, Beirut, his years at sea. I was so proud of him for following his conscience. Only later did I think of the danger he had placed us in: my mother and I as well as himself. But still I was proud.'

'We'll find him,' I said.

Low on fuel, we stopped at a filling station on the Budapest ring road. Iveta asked about the situation at the Hungarian/Serbia border and was told it was open, but to expect delays on the Serbian side. 'He thinks we're crazy. He thought we might get turned back. He said we would be better trying one of the quieter crossings. He mentioned

Kelebija or Tiszasziget as alternatives to the main Horgoš–Röszke post on the main road. Also, he said there'd be more traffic crossing over from the Serbian side. There are thousands of ethnic Hungarians wanting to get out of Serbia although it's been their home for generations.' She sighed. 'It's always that way isn't it.'

'Yes, it is. But those quieter crossings might arouse suspicion. I think we should stick to Horgoš–Röszke. Your IAEA ID should see us through.'

We'd agreed that I was simply her companion, an old friend whom she'd asked to accompany her as a safety measure under the prevailing circumstances. Her IAEA role was at the request of the UN, issued at short notice, which was why she had no official invitation. But she had observer status, which she assured me was not unusual in itself. It was flimsy but if it failed we had the Lloyd's Agent to fall back on. The Admiral had said Aleksandar Nenadovic, as part of a blue-blooded and still highly regarded Serb dynasty, carried weight in those parts. I'd have to take his word for it.

'Did you ask him about the security situation in Belgrade?' I asked her as we drove away.

'Yes, he thought it was quiet. The bombing has ended he said – for now at least.'

We pressed on, reaching the border at six in the morning. There were some tense moments on the Serb side while the border guards checked our papers and searched the car, but Iveta's ID helped and with traffic building all the time on the northbound crossing, the Serb guards were in danger of becoming overwhelmed. After some cursory questioning we were waved through and headed for Belgrade.

To my surprise, Iveta had GPS mapping in the car. She told me she loved exploring her new homeland. They hiked in the summer and skied in the winter. Her boyfriend had bought her the Tom Tom device recently for that purpose but we used it now as we entered the city's northern suburbs to locate Aleksandar's address in the old township of Zemun. We were both exhausted. Iveta, carrying the burden of her father's abduction on her shoulders, had become jumpy as well, not helped by the strong coffee we'd drunk through the night.

On the journey down I'd been giving thought to our meeting with Aleksandar. With their uncompromising nationalism, the Serbs were not winning any popularity contests on the international stage these days. Aleksandar Nenadovic was our only contact in this alien city and, despite the Admiral's reassurances, I wasn't sure what kind of welcome we'd get. I needn't have worried. He greeted us warmly as, having passed through wrought-iron gates and pulled up, we climbed the steps to his mansion. It stood in splendid isolation at the end of a leafy lane that served as a private drive, as there were no other houses nearby. Zemun was a maze of narrow streets crowded into a small area, yet this house stood like a citadel surrounded by its lowly cohorts.

'Welcome to this pitiful country,' he said, beaming. 'I am Aleksandar.' First he took Iveta's hand and bowing slightly, kissed it. Then he gripped my hand in both of his. 'I have spoken with the Admiral again, just this morning. He wanted to know whether you had arrived. Now I must call him. Come in, come in. Your luggage? You poor dears.' His English was precise, if somewhat old-world and heavily accented. He was somewhere in his sixties, tall and lean, his silver hair swept back off his forehead. But his eyebrows were black, his eyes blue and clear, and between them, a striking aquiline nose. He reminded me of the actor Christopher Lee.

We entered the house through a huge pair of doors leading into a dark, panelled hallway. We were led through into a brightly lit room at the back of the house on an equally grand scale as the hall. Sofas with faded oriental covers juxtaposed with well-worn leather Chesterfield wingchairs and an ottoman, all set on old carpets from Samarkand or Bokhara I imagined. Open French windows led out onto a paved terrace beyond which was a formally laid out garden stretching for a hundred yards or more down to the Danube. He ushered us to sit and served thick, sweet black coffee from small porcelain cups accompanied by a plate of crescent-shaped pastries filled with walnut and apple jam.

'Skaltsounia,' he said before sitting down himself. 'First, you will wash and rest. And don't worry, the caffeine has been boiled out of the coffee,' he added. 'My housekeeper is not here. I sent her back to her village away from the bombing, and I'm afraid my culinary skills are limited, so tonight I will take you to a restaurant just along the river where we will dine under the stars, though hopefully not the bombers!'

Charming host that he was, I did wonder when we would get to the subject matter, but I wasn't going to argue with him yet. Iveta was desperate too to pursue the search for her father, but we both needed to rest. He took us to our rooms. The shower was welcome and I slept dreamlessly until he woke us at seven that evening.

The Balkan Express was based around an old railway wagon set well above the Danube. We walked to the end of Zemun Quay and climbed a stairway up to the restaurant. A waiter with a black waxed moustache that Poirot would have been happy with seated us at a table outside with a view across the river. Strains of Romantic music wafted across the terrace and I asked Aleksandar what it was. 'The Serbs are a creative people, and that creativity extends far beyond the pen and the page. The history of our music is full with classical composers, but they have not received the credit they deserve.'

As we drank a local Muscat called *Tamjanika* and ate perch and bream cooked in a fish soup, Aleksandar told us about his life and his work. Here we were, enjoying excellent food and wine in good company, with a war raging around us and a nuclear warhead on the loose nearby.

'It's true I come from a noble family but there were plenty of rotten apples in the barrel too, I'm afraid. I was educated in England and joined a Lloyd's brokerage after I graduated. After seven years I returned to Belgrade, to the family home and the business my father had established in 1932.

'As the Committee of Lloyd's of London had stated when they established the network: "It is highly important to the interests of Underwriters, that a regular and universal system of intelligence and superintendence should be established in all the principal ports and places, both at home and abroad." I was introduced to your Admiral while still working in London. When this war broke out I was not surprised to hear from him and I have been reporting to him regularly throughout these tragic times.'

We let him talk. Iveta and I exchanged glances and I knew we were thinking the same thing: was he going to get to the purpose of our visit or should one of us jump in?

'Aleksandar . . .,' I began, but he had read our thoughts.

'And so my friends, here we are and I will tell you what I know, and what I fear. Then we can discuss what we are to do about it. I wanted you refreshed and well fed first, and to give you a little context.

'So, the IAEA's intelligence is partly correct: the *Phoenix Saturn* has transported this weapon, but not to Belgrade. She berthed at the port in Smederovo, forty-five kilometres downstream from here,' he gestured eastwards downriver. 'As you were on the road the vessel was approaching. She discharged her cargo before dawn and the amphibious vehicle, with its launcher, together with what we must presume is the nuclear missile camouflaged under a tarpaulin, are, as we sit here, heading south accompanied by an army truck of some kind.'

'So what are we sitting here for?' I asked.

'Because, my friend, I only learned of this minutes before I woke you this evening. It is better that you have rested and are prepared for what lies ahead. Anyway, these amphibious vehicles are only capable of travelling at fifty kilometres per hour and I have my people monitoring their progress minute by minute.'

It didn't surprise me that his 'people' could monitor the ship and the cargo's movements; it was what Lloyd's Agents did. But I was still impressed by the reach of his contacts and the efficiency of communications in a country that was, after all, at war.

'Which brings us,' he continued, 'to the questions: what is their destination, and once they reach it, what is their target?

'Do you know anything of Balkan history, and politics?' Neither of us replied. 'Then let me tell you. Don't worry, I will not attempt to educate you on the entire history of these troubled lands. But I must begin in 1389 when the Battle of Kosovo was fought and the Serbs were defeated. The battle took place on the 15th of June between the Serbs and an invading army of the Ottoman Empire. It was fought on the Kosovo Field in the territory ruled by a Serbian nobleman about five kilometres from what today is Kosovo's capital, Pristina. The bulk of both armies were wiped out and many of their senior commanders killed. The Serbs were left with too few men to defend their lands while the Turks had many more troops in the east to call upon. Consequently, the Serbian principalities that were not already Ottoman vassals became so in the following years.

'The defeat in battle is very important to Serbian history, to our traditions and our national identity. Some would say it has led to a national sense of victimhood. Without doubt, it scarred our nation. Today, Kosovo seeks independence and I believe it will and should have it, even if most Serbs would disagree. The truth is, we are oppressing the Kosovars, Kosovo's ethnic Albanian majority. The Kosovars have pursued a policy of peaceful resistance for several years but eventually they formed the Kosovo Liberation Army and an armed internal struggle followed. This, in turn, prompted Serbian security forces to conduct a massive military operation against the Kosovars, and 800,000 of them were forced out of their homes into neighbouring countries. And that is what has led to where we are now: NATO airstrikes.

'Now, as I said, the battle of 1389 was fought on the 15th of June. Today is the 13th. Yesterday we learned that NATO's KFOR peacekeeping force has entered Kosovo. There is still fighting going on there. And in three days' time it will be the 610th anniversary of the battle – of our national humiliation.'

Aleksandar paused.

'What are you saying?'

'I told you the convoy had left Smederevo and was heading south. My fear is that, aided – albeit under duress – by your father, Iveta, they plan to launch the missile from somewhere in the south of the country across the border to strike Pristina, the capital city of Kosovo and home to 200,000 people.'

Iveta stared at him. 'A nuclear strike against civilians and NATO troops in the heart of Europe?'

'Exactly.'

'Have you any idea who's behind this? Is it from within the Serbian state, the military, someone else?' I asked him.

'I cannot say for sure. Most likely it is one of several ultranationalist paramilitary organisations.'

'What's your best guess?'

'Well, if you asked me which of them has the closest ties with unsanctioned elements within Russian intelligence, then probably a shadowy figure known as the Kirurg, or the Surgeon. His connections would help explain how this weapon was acquired and transported so discreetly. And he is organised enough to pull it off.'

'He's a qualified surgeon, is he?'

'Well, who knows? He is said to have qualified in Magdeburg during the Communist era.'

'What else do you know about him?'

'You've heard of the Black Hand, I presume. Upon its formation in the early nineteen hundreds their objective was the unification of all the southern Slav states into one nation. It was headquartered in Belgrade, financed by the Serbian government and run by the head of Serb military intelligence at the time. Their aim was thwarted by the Habsburgs, rulers of the Austro-Hungarian Empire. And as I'm sure you know, the Black Hand's involvement in the assassination of Archduke Franz Ferdinand in the summer of 1914 precipitated the First World War.'

'Yes, but I thought it fell apart after they'd bumped him off.'

'It did, more or less. But remember, the Black Hand was always a secret society so perhaps we should not be surprised if it still exists and has been resuscitated clandestinely. We have several such paramilitary movements in Serbia – the White Eagles for example – with not dissimilar aims. But these people, the Black Hand I mean, are widely rumoured to have support from Russia in the shape of the GRU, unsanctioned or otherwise; hence their ability to get hold of this dreadful weapon. And we must beware lest history should repeat itself.'

'But do you actually know it is them, or are you guessing?' asked Iveta.

'It is what I have heard. The Surgeon, who is now the self-appointed leader of the Black Hand, is no regular warlord. Apparently he is well educated, a charismatic man, but stays in the shadows. He is enigmatic, but myths and legends often form around such characters so let us not jump to conclusions.'

'But you believe these are the same people who have kidnapped my father?'

'Yes, I believe so. And that is enough for now, my young friends. Tomorrow we must travel south to find them.'

The warm night, the stars, the music, the wine and the company of this charming character had done nothing to lessen the gravity of the situation. We walked back to Aleksandar's house and with a weary wave Iveta headed for her room.

'She will sleep well,' said Aleksandar before pouring me a small glass of slivovitz. 'I couldn't say this in front of her but you may know that much of the Stasi were headquartered in Magdeburg. They locked up over ten thousand political prisoners there right up until the fall of the GDR and I have heard that the Kirurg helped them develop their "enhanced" interrogation techniques. This is hearsay, but he was involved with the Stasi, that much is known. And by all accounts the Stasi's interrogation methods were every bit as merciless as those of the Nazis. In any event, he is said to be a very dangerous man: an ultranationalist driven by dreams of a greater Serbia and a fanatical hatred of the Kosovars who themselves, of course, dream of unification to form a greater Albania: once again a threat from Islam.

We have many such people with similar nationalistic dreams, and harbouring such hatreds.'

Chapter 21

Belgrade - Golija Mountains, Serbia

13 June 1999

Early the next morning over breakfast Aleksandar announced his plans. By his reckoning there were only two likely locations from which the missile could be launched: the mountain ranges of Kopaonik or Golija.

'My guess is Golija,' he said. 'Kopaonik is very popular with tourists – in winter for the skiing, but in summer too with hikers, even now despite the war. So is Golija, but it is more remote and heavily forested so provides cover. There is a monastery on the northern flank, the Monastery of Ravanica. We should head there first and speak to the monks. They may have seen or heard something.'

'We need to get all this back to the Admiral,' I said. 'Including what you told us last night – your theories and your reasons.'

He smiled. 'Already done. I sent him a full report by fax after you had gone to bed. I told him where we were heading so he'll know where to look for us.'

He seemed to be thinking of everything.

We arrived in the late afternoon, drawing up beside a fortified gate, part of a circular wall that enclosed the monastery's various chapels and residences. We'd got out of

Aleksandar's ageing Saab, stretching after the non-stop eight-hour journey when a black-robed monk with a white beard down to his chest emerged through a small door set within the main gate. As Aleksandar engaged him in conversation Iveta and I moved away from the heat into the shade cast by the wall.

'I am so anxious,' she sighed. 'How do we know we are in the right place? They could be anywhere. It is like searching for a pin in a haystack.'

'If anyone can find them it's this guy,' I said, to offer her some hope. But we both knew Aleksandar's plans were based only on a hunch that Pristina was the target and that we were looking in the right place for the missile, and for Valdis.

He walked over to us, the monk trailing behind him. 'He is Father Jovan. He says they have seen nothing, but he will ask some of the shepherds who come down from the mountain in the evenings for their supper in the monastery. He has asked us to join him and his brothers inside.'

'I don't want to waste time here!' Iveta suddenly exploded. 'How do we know they are even on this mountain, or whether this old man or the shepherds can find them?'

'I understand your impatience, my dear, but have a little faith. My instincts rarely fail me.' From the moment we'd met him Aleksandar had exuded a calm confidence which reassured even me, but Iveta was getting more and more edgy, and I could understand why. What had not been said, but what we were all wondering, was whether Valdis had been broken? Was he still alive, even?

We followed the monk through the gate and into a courtyard shaded by the high surrounding walls and lines of tall, slender cypress trees. From somewhere within came the sound of chanting. The place provided an occasional refuge for hikers and we were assured we were not intruding. 'They've asked for a donation too,' said Aleksandar, 'towards the upkeep. The Orthodox Church is short of funds nowadays, apparently.'

We were shown to our cells and told of the monastery's routine, which we were asked to respect. We washed, rested for an hour, then gathered in the courtyard.

'The shepherds usually arrive shortly after nightfall,' said Aleksandar, 'so we have an hour or so. We can talk to them as we eat together.'

Iveta was even more impatient by now. 'We should be searching the mountain *now*.'

'No,' I said, 'he's right. The shepherds know these hills and will know who comes and goes.'

The first shepherd arrived as night was falling, just as Father Jovan had predicted. He had seen no sign of a military convoy, and so it was with the second old fellow. They were eager to talk among themselves and we left them to it, eating our food at a separate table. We finished the *pljeskavica*, the Balkan version of a hamburger topped with a form of cream made from sheep's milk. This was washed down with jugs of the monks' own wine, which was rough and welcome.

It was almost midnight when the third man came down from the hills. He was younger than the other two, in his early forties, and displayed a nervous energy. He immediately began regaling Father Jovan with a story. Aleksandar listened, then got up and walked over to where the two men were conversing. It was obvious that the shepherd had seen something out of the ordinary and was giving his account unbidden. After a while Aleksandar returned to where we were sitting, visibly excited.

'We are in luck! His name is Falkon. He's been watching the convoy since it arrived. The transporter, covered in tarpaulins, has been positioned on the southern flank of Jankov Kamen, the highest peak in this range. They would have travelled through the night and arrived this afternoon along with a support vehicle – a Zastava army truck – a group including drivers and a commander; and another man, not in uniform. They have set up camp. They're dressed in battle fatigues and wearing black berets. It's heavily forested up there and he was able to get close enough to see that their tunics carried a badge showing a skull and crossbones. That was the insignia of the Black Hand. It's the byname of *Ujedinjenje ili Smrt,* meaning Union or Death.'

'Death to whom? Do they mean do or die themselves, or death to those who resist?' I asked.

'The latter. And so this confirms our suspicions.'

'Can he guide us to the camp? Is he reliable?'

'For a fee, yes he can, and yes I believe he is reliable. He's a Vlach. They've been practising transhumance in these ranges for centuries – bringing their flocks up to the summer pastures in late spring, then moving them back to their lowland villages for the winter. They are family-owned flocks of two or three hundred sheep, run by a man and his wife or a man and his brother or nephew, not the huge pastoral groups of the old days.'

I looked at Falkon as Aleksandar spoke. He was a rough-looking character, short and square-shouldered, strong with a broad brow, a bony nose and sharp eyes. As I observed him he returned my stare with one of his own: challenging and a little belligerent. I wouldn't have wanted to get on the wrong side of him.

'The Vlachs speak a language closely related to Latin and to today's Romanian. I can barely understand a word but he also speaks Serbo-Croat well, and a very little English too.'

'And did you tell him they plan to attack Pristina?'

'He's uneducated of course, but not stupid. Vlachs don't harbour the same grudge against the Kosovars as I'm afraid my countrymen do. He was genuinely angry when I told him what we believe is happening, and that the Black Hand are involved. Of course he knows about them and their role in Serbian history. He will help us. Oh, and he wanted to know who you were. Were you the woman's husband, he asked, and were you in charge? I told him no, you weren't, but yes you were in charge.'

'Okay. So then what?' I asked, as much to myself as to him. 'We're not just going to walk up the mountain and ask them to call it off, are we? Are you, Iveta, me and him going to take them on? What are our chances?'

We were on our own. Our Nokias were useless up here, and the monastery had no phone of any description.

'These, my friend, are reasonable questions. We have twenty-four hours. We have no outside help to call on, but the stakes are too high and time is too short to turn our backs on this now. It could be that we have to make sacrifices, perhaps the ultimate sacrifice if it means our lives in exchange for those 200,000 in Pristina. We are placing ourselves in harm's way.'

Chapter 22

Mount Jankov Kamen, Golija Range, Southern Serbia

14-15 June 1999

We rose at dawn and after a meagre breakfast prepared by the monks, and with rucksacks Aleksandar had brought with him containing thick winter sweaters, headed on foot into the hills following our guide, Falkon. He had stayed overnight in the monastery and now strode ahead of us. Soon we were climbing up through heavily shaded beech woods, the earth thick with their fallen leaves from the winter. The ground rose steeply now. Iveta was fit and well rested making light work of the climb. Like her, I was wearing trainers barely suitable for the conditions, but when I saw the old *opanci* sandals Falkon was wearing I considered myself well off. Aleksandar was struggling and we had to stop every fifteen minutes or so to wait for him to catch up. Along the way we drank from cold mountain streams and ate wedges of crusty bread with sheep's cheese that the monks had provided.

Eventually the beech woods gave way to pines, the strong scent of their resin heavy in the mounting heat. We sweated, and rested for short periods on soft beds of pine needles. From time to time we could look down and see the monastery far below. Above us eagles circled effortlessly on the thermals, their cries a persistent exchange of *kwits* and *kees*. We were in a dreamlike pastoral Arcadia, yet there was little joy to it, only a sense of foreboding.

We climbed on until, as darkness was falling, we reached a sloping alpine meadow carpeted in wild flowers on the far edge of which was the shepherds' camp: a gathering of huts, or *bačija* as Falkon called them. As we approached, an older man emerged from one of them. It was much colder now. We were over 1,800 metres above sea level and he wore a voluminous cape of thick black hair topped by a strange, conical-shaped felt hat. He was introduced to us as Falkon's father. He was accompanied by two enormous dogs wearing collars ringed with three inch-long steel spikes. These beasts were guard dogs used not to round up but to protect the flock. They were used too by the Serb police, and increasingly as domestic pets by macho city boys. The spiked collars protected their throats from attack by wolves that roamed these mountains. The dogs barked aggressively, though more in greeting than belligerence, Falkon insisted.

This wasn't all Falkon had to say. 'He says it's not just wolves they protect against,' explained Aleksandar. 'There are sheep rustlers in the mountains too. They come up here in big pickup trucks. If they encounter the dogs they'll shoot them.'

'And what if they encounter the shepherds?'

Aleksandar translated my question and Falkon glared over at me as he answered in English: 'We shoot *them*. Then we cut their throats.' As if I needed an explanation he drew a finger across his. 'We kill seven of them in one night last year. Put them in back of pickup and take them down to Novi Pazar. Leave them on the street. No trouble since.' I was simultaneously horrified and reassured.

After we'd rested and devoured bowls of fried noodles prepared for us by the family matriarch, we took off again, guided by Falkon and heading to the higher ground where he'd seen the transporter the previous day. Falkon and I carried old SKS carbines, semi-automatic and each with a twenty-round magazine that his father had handed to us. His younger brother, Ilijan, had wanted to join us but his wife resisted. She'd given birth to their first child only weeks before and wanted him at home.

It was three in the morning of the 15th when we reached the summit of Jankov Kamen. The day of the battle's anniversary. A rain storm, accompanied by thunder and lightning, had blown in unannounced from the north, soaking us and turning the rutted track we were on into a slippery morass made worse by the trenches the heavy transporter had gouged out when it had come this way. The squall passed clearing the sky but leaving the ground saturated and the trees, and us, dripping.

Now, we looked down from the summit onto the mountain's southern flank where, lit by the moonlight and protruding from a clearing in the pine trees, we could make out the sharp-nosed missile pointing south towards Kosovo, towards Pristina, the capital city that we now knew was its target. It looked incongruous and sinister in the ethereal beauty of that silvery setting. The fickle mountain winds had swung round now to blow from the south. It brought with it the smell of a fire we could see smoking in the centre of the camp. And it carried the sound of voices too – murmurings punctuated by the occasional outburst of shouting and laughter. One man was fanning the fire, trying to coax the damp wood into flames. I wondered whether they'd been drinking, and if so how heavily. Enough to make them careless? I got the answer when another one stood over the fire and poured a bottle of something onto it. A moment later it caught and flames leapt high into the night. The two men jumped backwards, roaring with laughter.

'That is high-proof stuff they've been drinking to go up like that,' whispered Aleksandar.

We'd come up here to retrieve Valdis. By rescuing him we would be able to prevent the missile's launch. No Valdis meant no PAL code, and no launch. We'd more or less ruled out any attempt at negotiating with the Surgeon and his Black Hand gang. They had to be neutralised we'd decided, by whatever means available. Between us we had the advantage of height and the element of surprise. But little else. We could see we were outnumbered, and they would have superior weaponry against our carbines. They had Valdis as a hostage to bargain with too.

Alcksandar had briefed Falkon following what he and I had discussed the previous evening. Now we were here we had to decide how best to implement our hastily conceived and theoretical assault plan. With hindsight it was foolhardy to have thought we had much chance in the first place. The stakes were too high. But we couldn't do nothing, and we had no means of calling in help from the outside world; none of which made it any less irksome when our sketchy plan went so wrong. But who could blame Iveta for what she did? We'd been there for ten minutes, watching, assessing the situation. Aleksandar was scanning the camp through an old pair of field glasses he'd brought with him. Suddenly he whispered harshly: 'My God, is that him? Your father? He's tied to a chair. Sweet Jesus, they're not putting him in the fire!'

Before I could reach for the glasses Iveta grabbed them, focusing on the scene below. Then, throwing them aside, she broke cover taking off down the steep slope towards the camp, slipping in the mud, her arms flailing.

I reached down and picked up the glasses from where she'd dropped them. Now I watched as she rushed towards the camp where her father was struggling, the chair on its side and Valdis tied to it, lying half in and half out of the fire. And she was already halfway down the slope.

'Time to use these?' Falkon asked, holding up his carbine. 'Come, we get better shot over there.'

I told Aleksandar to wait where he was and, seeking cover among the trees, we ran over to the west side of the camp. From here the whole site was exposed, while we were concealed among the pines. Finding a vantage point, we dropped to lie prone on the ground, carbines resting on our rucksacks, stocks pressed into our shoulders.

The scene below was confused. Iveta had reached her father and was trying to pull him out of the fire. A man was standing on the opposite side of the fire, arms folded, legs apart, unarmed. Was this who they called Kirurg, the Surgeon? He was tall and heavily built. His fatigues were neatly pressed, his black jackboots shining and his black beret precisely positioned on his large head with the badge positioned above his left eye. An armband clearly displayed the Black Hand's skull and crossbones insignia. There was no question who was in command. Now though, his manner seemed more one of curiosity than command at what was happening before him: Valdis struggling and groaning loudly amid the flames as Iveta managed to drag him out, showing the hysterical strength of someone acting in desperation.

Either side of where the Surgeon stood were two men also in fatigues, both cradling automatic rifles. The Surgeon had raised his hand now and was speaking, though I couldn't make out what he was saying. Iveta looked up. She'd managed to drag her father a few yards away from the fire. Now she stood up, facing the Surgeon defiantly. The wind had strengthened. Clouds swept across the moon and the fire's flames, fanned by the wind, leapt and soared into the night, casting shadows that shifted and wavered in a scene from a gothic nightmare, the dark forest providing a macabre backdrop.

The Surgeon's two guards were as big as him and stood close in either side. If we were to take out the Surgeon, we'd have to take out the guards first. 'We take the two either side of the Kirurg.' I spoke softly. 'Shoot the one on his far side and I'll take the nearest. Single shots.' Falkon would be the better shot, I was sure of that. 'Then we both aim for the Kirurg. There must be more but I can only see one beside the fire. Try for him as well but he's close to the old man and the girl, so be careful. There'll be others down by the vehicles. They'll come up when we start shooting. Ready?'

We fired simultaneously. Falkon struck his target with his first shot. I fired hitting mine with my second and third shots. Both men fell but the Surgeon was quick. Instead of running down to the vehicles as I'd hoped he might, he leapt round the fire and seized Iveta. I fired and missed. Neither of us could get a clear shot at him. To add to the chaos, Aleksandar was running down towards the camp. He was shouting but I couldn't catch what he was saying. He reached them. Valdis lay on the ground, motionless, and the Surgeon held Iveta round the neck, shielding himself with her body. The other man, the one who'd poured spirit on the fire, now moved to cover Valdis with his weapon, crouching down beside him. Aleksandar stood before them, gesticulating as he spoke. It looked as though, in desperation he was trying to negotiate, to reason with the Surgeon, Serb to Serb. But the Surgeon was holding the cards. As with the GRU crow – how many days ago now? – I'd made a mistake in thinking he wasn't armed. He'd drawn a pistol and was holding it to Iveta's ear. She had no way to resist.

Falkon held up a hand, cocking his head. 'Listen,' he whispered. The sound of an engine. I could see it now: the Zastava truck climbing the hill up from where it would have been parked further down the meadow alongside the missile transporter. Its headlights blazed, throwing a harsh, brilliant light across the site, catching the figures as frozen silhouettes.

It stopped short of the fire and the driver and another man got out. Then shots rang out, hitting the front of the truck. One of its headlights was hit and died with a hissing sound. The driver and his passenger crouched down beside their vehicle, using it as a shield, unsure where the firing was coming from. It only gave them cover from our side, but I couldn't see who was shooting either. Whoever it was, they were opposite us on the eastern side of the camp.

There was another single shot and a loud scream. The Zastava's passenger lay on the ground clawing at the grass in a vain attempt to get up and escape. Another shot, and now he lay still. Three down, at least three remaining: the Surgeon, who had Iveta, the driver and the man by the fire guarding Valdis – only now he had Aleksandar too, pinned to the ground with his boot on his neck.

The Surgeon spoke to him and he released Aleksandar and returned to Valdis, pulling the chair upright, lifting his head up by the hair and slapping him until he regained some level of consciousness. Now the Surgeon, still holding the pistol, lifted Iveta bodily, holding her struggling in his arms like a disobedient child, and stepped towards the fire.

'Old man,' he shouted, his voice clearly audible now above the wind. 'You think you are strong to resist me, but now? Your daughter's turn. You want to watch her burn alive? So it is her or the Muslim dirt of Pristina? What is your choice, old man? Decide! The code or your child?'

Iveta fought desperately as Valdis, alert now, realised the terrifying dilemma he faced: surrender the launch code, save Iveta, but condemn the people of the Kosovan capital to death; or watch his cherished daughter suffer an agonising end before his eyes and save the city. How do you make a choice like that?

It had all happened so fast. Now I stared down at the scene, knowing I had to act. Falkon was looking at me, waiting as I hesitated, cursing my own indecision. It was a standoff, but it wouldn't last forever. The Surgeon moved closer to the fire. Then, as if making a sacrificial offering to the gods, he looked up at the night sky. But it wasn't their blessing he was seeking. Clouds had covered the moon and the rain had begun again – a gentle patter at first but within seconds it had intensified into another torrential downpour. Now the only light came from the truck's remaining headlight as the rain beat down, dowsing the fire's flames. It didn't take long for the Surgeon to realise that it had dowsed his chance too. The fire was hissing loudly as it died and with it his bargaining chip. But he still had them both: father and daughter.

He dropped Iveta to the ground but still held onto her, keeping her on her feet with his arm round her neck, the pistol to her temple. The Surgeon shouted something at the man holding Valdis, then turned and began heading towards the truck, using Iveta as his shield. For a moment they were both illuminated by the Zastava's single headlight cutting through the rain. Another shot rang out – a single round, again fired from the other side of the camp.

'Ilijan!' whispered Falkon. 'I knew it was him!'

Maybe it was a just a warning, for neither Ilijan, Falkon nor myself could get a clear shot at the Surgeon without risking Iveta's life. He'd reached the truck now and pushed Iveta into the cab before climbing into the driver's seat alongside her. He killed the headlight and in the darkness turned and began descending the slope. I fired hoping to hit its engine or its tires but it kept moving. The driver who'd brought it up to the clearing no longer had cover and was running down the hill after it. Again it was Ilijan who picked him off. The man's arms flew up and he pitched forward into the mud.

Aleksandar was unarmed, guarded by the remaining Black Hand gangster. Valdis was not moving, either unconscious or dead, and neither Falkon nor his brother could get a clear shot at that one remaining man, Valdis's tormenter. The scene that had been so brightly illuminated by the fire, the headlight and the moon, was now in darkness. I moved down the slope towards the fire, my carbine raised.

But I was only halfway down when I heard a dog baying. I froze as I watched the beast charging down into the clearing from the eastern side, Ilijan's side. I raised the rifle to my shoulder, but the tormenter was armed too. He stepped forward and fired wildly before, seeing the dog bounding towards him, panicked, taking off down the slope in the direction of the Zastava, which was now out of sight. Whether the hound acted instinctively in pursuit of the running man, or whether Ilijan had instructed it, I never found out. It swerved and, as it approached the fleeing figure, leapt, landing across the man's shoulders and back, bringing him tumbling to the ground. This was no police dog trained to apprehend but not injure its target. It was trained to kill wolves and intruders. The man's scream was choked off as the dog's powerful jaws closed round his throat. For a few moments he tried to wrestle with it, twisting and turning to free himself from the dog's teeth. Then he lay still. I watched as the dog prowled round the lifeless body, sniffing the blood, until Ilijan approached and called it off.

There was no sound now except for the rain and the rustling of the wind in the pines. Even the dog was silent. I walked down to the firepit, where Aleksandar was crouching beside Valdis.

'How is he?' I asked.

'I don't think he will live.'

Valdis was unconscious, his breathing shallow, his pulse fast and where it hadn't burned, his skin was clammy and cold. Most of his clothing, his shoes and one side of his face and body were burned, the skin red or charred. 'We need to get him back to your camp,' I said, addressing the two brothers. 'Then off the mountain, to a hospital. You have transport?'

'We can find something,' Falkon said.

'Where's the nearest town with a hospital?'

'Novi Pazar. It's thirty kilometres south of here. But it will take time to drive off the mountain. It is just a track.'

'What about the missile?' Aleksandar asked.

'They can't fire it now. We need to contact the Admiral. It needs military intervention. But first we get Valdis to a hospital.' It was the only consolation: at least we'd prevented the thing being launched – for now. The anniversary of the battle had come but the moment had passed and been pushed back six hundred years into the mists of time. I still felt sick: Valdis dying, Iveta captured by a maniac and taken God knows where. Did he think he could still use her as a lever to get at the code? Maybe it would be better if Valdis did die, and the code with him.

I looked around at the carnage and thought of the score I had still to settle. And at that moment the gods bestowed on us their climax to the night's events : a jagged fork of lightning pierced the sky followed seconds later by an ear-slitting clap of thunder.

I turned to Aleksandar, Falkon and his brother: 'Let's get him out of here.'

Chapter 23

Novi Pazar General Hospital

15 June 1999

It took us six hours to come down off that bloody mountain and on to the hospital at Novi Pazar. The ancient van we were travelling in belonged to the shepherds, and it smelled like it. The track was heavily rutted and flooded from the downpours. We were heading downhill, which hastened our descent, but on several occasions we slid and were in danger of plunging over the side. Falkon was driving and was confronting the urgency of the situation with a zeal bordering on recklessness. We'd dropped Ilijan off at the camp and between us Aleksandar and I kept Valdis as comfortable as we could, removing some of his clothing and laying damp pieces of cloth over the worst of his burns. We laid a woollen blanket over him and Aleksandar had painkillers which, with difficulty, we got him to swallow. He drifted in and out of consciousness but even when vaguely responsive his mutterings were incoherent. At one point he became agitated and shouted Iveta's name. At the hospital Falkon left us, saying he would return to the monastery. I carried Valdis in my arms into the reception area, where we waited while Aleksandar spoke to a young duty doctor.

The fact that we'd averted a nuclear attack hardly seemed to matter at that moment. We sat in silence, exhausted, Valdis still in my arms, Aleksandar beside me. The minutes passed before our gloomy contemplation was broken as someone shouted my name. I looked up to see the Admiral walking down the corridor. Even more of a surprise was his companion. Dr Kirstin Mackenzie hurried up to us and knelt to examine Valdis.

'God, you're a sight for sore eyes. How the …?'

'Later, Angus. We need to get him into a ward where we can treat him.'

At this point a young orderly arrived wheeling a trolley. I gently laid Valdis on it and the two of them disappeared down the corridor followed by the Admiral who returned after a few minutes.

He sighed. 'Doesn't look good I'm afraid. What happened up there? Are you alright, Aleksandar? Good to see you again, even in these dire circumstances. And I'm grateful for your interventions.'

'We'll tell you,' I said, 'but is there anywhere round here we can get a coffee and something to eat?'

Aleksandar hailed a passing orderly who eventually returned with three cups of lukewarm coffee and a plate of greasy burgers, these topped with raw onions and tomatoes. As we ate we gave our account of events.

'So the missile is still up there?'

'Yes,' I said. 'And the Surgeon has Iveta and is no doubt preparing his ultimatum as we sit here discussing it. He'll be assuming he can still offer Iveta's freedom in return for the code. Aleksandar, can you call one of your informants to see if they can track them down? I doubt they've gone back up the mountain. More likely they've hightailed it back to some Black Hand hideout in Belgrade. We never saw it but I've been wondering if he had the PAL controller with him in the truck when he drove off.'

'It would have been an aluminium or steel case – the size of an attaché case,' said the Admiral. We continued speculating as to the Surgeon's next move and our own course of action until Kirstin came back along the corridor. She looked first at the Admiral, then turned to me. 'There was nothing we could do,' she said, touching my arm.

'He's dead.' I couldn't quite believe it.

'I know how close you were. I'm so sorry.'

'As we'd feared,' the Admiral sighed. 'I'm sorry too, old boy. We'll need to arrange for his body to be removed from here. More immediately, we need to find his daughter.

Now there was a signal, Aleksandar was speaking on his phone. 'They'll get back to me,' he said after finishing the call. 'It's a conspicuous vehicle. They'll check the Black Hand's haunts both in Belgrade and Smederovo.'

I turned to Kirstin. 'What killed him? The shock?' I remembered seeing the results of a crankcase explosion on three engineroom crew who'd suffered third and fourth degree burns. Cause of death had been stated as shock, but that was after a huge explosion. Valdis had suffered terribly, but he hadn't been subjected to that kind of blast.

'I believe so,' said Kirstin. 'Death is most often caused by shock in fatal cases of burn injury – cardiogenic shock. Lung injury may have played a part too. We can't be sure and you weren't there earlier while he was being tortured. There may have been other contributing injures. I don't think we can expect any dependable post-mortem examination here.' She turned to the Admiral. 'It's best to get him somewhere where a proper autopsy can be carried out.'

'We'll take care of that,' he replied. 'And any decision on where a funeral will take place rather depends on Iveta, if and when you find her, poor girl. I would counsel against Latvia under the circumstances, but it would be up to her.'

'Alright. We need to get back to the monastery to pick up Aleksandar's car,' I said. 'And we need to be certain the bastard hasn't taken her back up the mountain with him.'

As Aleksandar summoned a taxi I took Kirstin to one side and we exchanged awkward small talk. Over the past days she'd appeared in my thoughts unbidden: at the recital, at the Balkan Express restaurant, on the climb up through the forests of the Jankov Kamen mountain. Those thoughts had been a balm on my troubled mind. To see her now, even under these circumstances, was almost overwhelming, but there was too much else going on, and too little time for us to return to the ease we'd fallen into so quickly in Scotland.

***

As we pulled up outside the monastery courtyard, Falkon appeared accompanied by his brother. His first words were, 'It has gone.'

'The missile?', I asked, as if I didn't know.

'Yes, rocket. It has gone. Transporter still there, but rocket has gone. Also, Ilijan was in the *bačija* and heard helicopter circling round summit. He saw it too. Big helicopter. Then it disappeared. Must have landed. He heard it again but didn't see it this time. He went back to their camp this morning. Only truck there – transporter, I mean. No rocket.'

I guessed the Surgeon would have got word to his GRU friends who'd arranged to bring the weapon into Serbia in the first place. You don't conjure up a heavy-lift chopper out of thin air without military contacts to organise it. At least the missile had not been armed.

'That seals it then,' stated Aleksandar. 'He will have taken her to Belgrade or Smederovo, one or the other, but we try Belgrade first. Agree?'

'Agreed.'

Father Jovan had joined us. We thanked him and Falkon and bade them goodbye, and in Aleksandar's Saab began the long drive back to the capital.

'I'll take the first leg,' I volunteered, 'but if you see me driving with my eyes shut give me a nudge.'

'You mean if I'm not asleep myself.'

We were approaching the outskirts of Belgrade when we picked up a phone signal again. We stopped and called the Admiral. I told him of the missile's disappearance, but he already knew. 'The intelligence we have suggests it's been taken back to Abkhazia. That's unconfirmed but the chopper was seen heading eastwards from the Bulgarian coast. What's your ETA Belgrade?'

'We're almost there.'

'Let me know when you've located Iveta and the Surgeon and I'll arrange for a team to take over.'

'Don't you mean if?'

He ignored that. 'We have access to a NATO unit now. They're standing by, awaiting my instructions. Just don't try and take the Surgeon on yourself.'

It sounded fine in theory. All we had to do was find them, call the Admiral and he'd send in a handy little team of commandos to rescue Iveta and finish off the Surgeon. For a moment I let myself believe that was the way it would happen.

Chapter 24

Belgrade

16 June 1999

It was pitch-black down here. Aleksandar had a pocket torch, but it provided only a faint and narrow beam to guide us through the puddles and potholes. The concrete floor had rotted over the years since the Germans had restored this medieval network of tunnels beneath the ancient Kalemegdan Fortress. The stronghold had been used by the city's various rulers: Celts, Romans, then Huns, Slavic tribes, Byzantines, Hungarians, Ottoman Turks, Austrians and more recently, Germans, as they all sought to control the meeting point of the Sava and Danube rivers, and so hold the gateway to Europe. And over those centuries, a maze of underground passages, fortifications, bunkers and command posts had been carved.

'In 1944 German troops were trying to break the contact between the partisans and the Red Army which was moving towards the city,' Aleksandar told me, his voice low. 'No one's sure how long they were down here for or how many escaped. The city was liberated and the Germans vanished into the building where we just came in, on the corner of Nemanjina Street. But for days afterwards the odd German soldier would appear from the tunnels and fire a few rounds or toss a hand grenade then vanish again. They were persistent.'

It was on Nemanjina Street that we'd located the Zastava truck parked outside an old building – the one used by the Germans and through which we'd found our way down here. Aleksandar's informer had guided us there based on a reliable source who was certain it was used by the Black Hand to access the tunnels. The building itself was deserted but we'd discovered the entrance to the tunnel through a door in the basement. It was the smell of sweat mingled with the faintest scent of a woman's perfume that had persuaded us that Iveta had been brought this way. I thought I was imagining it until Aleksandar said he could detect the scent too. Now we were feeling our way along a warren of underground tunnels, dugouts and chambers, never sure whether we were heading in the right direction. I was beginning to worry that we weren't when Aleksandar stopped abruptly and held up his hand. I could hear it too now: away from the dripping water and the occasional scurrying of rats, was the sound of voices. We moved even more cautiously now. Towards the raised voices of two men speaking loudly.

'Wait here,' I whispered.

'No, you will need me.'

I held his arm. 'Wait here and follow me after I've seen what's going on in there.'

'No. Let me speak to them first. Then you can intervene.'

I hesitated. 'Okay,' I said, compromising, 'we'll go in together.' There was no point in standing there arguing, but I could see that Aleksandar was almost dropping with exhaustion. I wasn't far off myself.

The room was big, the air fetid and damp. A single light bulb hung from the ceiling illuminating walls covered in a wet, greenish mould. I learned later that German troops had used it as a dormitory and I could imagine it would have been able to accommodate twenty or more beds. It reminded me of White Swan. Now its only occupants were two men and a woman. The Surgeon was standing arguing with another man who was dressed in camouflage fatigues. Whatever they were talking about, the discussion was heated. The woman – I could see it was Iveta – was lying on the floor against a wall, hands secured behind her back, her ankles shackled by heavy irons and thick grey tape covering her mouth. Her jeans were filthy from the mud on the mountain. The sweater she'd been wearing was gone and her thin top had been ripped open. An image flashed through my mind of her in a black evening gown on the night of the recital. She had banished her nerves, performed faultlessly and afterwards, for a few brief minutes, enjoyed the praise of an admiring audience. Then her world turned upside down. Now, although she didn't know it, her father was dead. And she had no mother or siblings to go back to either.

I'd rehearsed a line: 'Hands above your head,' I would shout, the old SKS raised to my shoulder. But the Surgeon's accomplice thought he'd beat me to it. As we entered he reached inside his jacket. I didn't wait to see what it was - cigarettes maybe, or a wallet? I doubted that so I fired intuitively, holding the rifle butt against my hip. It was a wild shot, the carbine awkward to handle in such a confined space. But it hit him and he went sprawling as the force of the round knocked him off balance. The Surgeon froze. Aleksandar shouted at him and very slowly he raised his arms. I kept the carbine on him as Aleksandar moved over to where Iveta lay. She was struggling, nodding her head frantically. He ripped the tape from her mouth. She took a desperate gulp of air and, between coughing spasms, gasped: 'He's got the keys, the one you shot.' Aleksandar crossed the room to get the keys and in doing so cut across the line of fire I had on the Surgeon. He saw his chance and bolted, heading for the door in the far corner of the room. I took a shot at him and missed, the bullet making a high-pitched whine as it ricocheted of the wall. I followed him, realising too late that his accomplice was down but not out. He'd drawn a gun and was aiming it at me. Aleksandar, himself unarmed, ran to disarm him. Anticipating it, the man changed the direction of his aim. I swung round and fired twice as he lay on the floor, but I was too late. He'd loosed off a quick, hit-or-miss round as he lay dying, but it was enough to bring Aleksandar down.

I went back and bent over him. The shot had caught him in his right side. Now he lay doubled-up, hugging himself tightly as if to make the pain go away. I looked around, hoping to find anything that might help him. Iveta was shouting. I turned back to the man who lay still now, dark blood spreading out around him onto the rough stone floor. Yet another bloody corpse in a growing count. I found a bunch of keys in the man's pocket, ran back to Iveta and fumbled with them until I'd unbound her wrists and unlocked the leg irons.

'Is there anything here? A medicine cabinet? Painkillers?'

'Just that rucksack. Over there,' she said pointing over at the door. I helped her to her feet, not sure whether to attend to her, to Aleksandar or go after the Surgeon.

From across the room Aleksandar was rasping something. We went over to where he lay and between us eased open his jacket and shirt to see the wound. The bullet had torn through his side between the bottom of his ribcage and around where I guessed his right kidney would be. It could have punctured a lung, a kidney or some other organ, or if he was lucky, just passed through skin and muscle. There wasn't much blood and his breathing and pulse were steady. But having seen how Valdis had succumbed, and given that Aleksandar was a similar age, I worried now that shock might set in.

'Don't concern yourself,' he whispered. 'It really is not a serious wound, I can tell.' How could he possibly know how serious it was?

'Angus, go after him,' he whispered urgently. 'Now. He will make for the river, I am sure. I believe there's a central culvert into which other streams run. Follow the water down the incline and you may find him. Iveta will look after me, but you must not let him get away or he will continue with his insane plan. And Angus, don't worry, I will tell her.'

At that moment Iveta brought over the rucksack. Now she pulled it open and spread the contents onto the floor, producing two plastic bottles of water, a can of beer and a small steel hip flask. I unscrewed the cap and sniffed it: slivovitz. There were also some magazines, a grubby-looking hand towel and a black flag with a crude rendering of the Black Hand's Union or Death insignia set around the skull and crossbones.

'Give him water and some of the spirit to drink, and to clean the wound. And use this as a bandage,' I added ripping the flag into strips.

'Don't worry,' she reassured me. 'I will bandage the wound and make him comfortable. Go now.'

I looked at her. I had no idea what had happened from the time she was dragged away from the fire on the mountain; what she'd had to endure. I went over and removed the gun from the dead man's hand.

'I'll be back. Look after him.'

'Of course she will,' Aleksandar muttered. I didn't envy him having to tell her of her father's death.

The tunnel into which the Surgeon had escaped was no more than five feet high by three feet wide. Its stone floor was smooth, wet and slippery. Stooping, and with the torch's weak beam to guide me, I moved down the incline. He was at least five minutes ahead of me, and he would guess that he'd be followed. After a hundred yards the tunnel opened out at a junction with two others. I took the wider of the two. This tunnel was a culvert: wider and higher, but with water running down it a foot deep. And the further down I went, the steeper the slope became. Several times I slipped. The first time this happened I lost the torch, but as my eyes became accustomed to the darkness I detected a faint light far ahead. I had the dead man's gun and drew it now, stopping to familiarise myself with it. It still had thirteen 9mm rounds left in the magazine. I continued edging my way down the tunnel.

The noise of rushing water made it impossible to listen for any other sound so I had no warning when he sprang out from a recess in the tunnel wall. We tumbled to the floor, each grappling to get a hold of the other but slithering down the progressively steeper incline in fast-flowing water, our rate of descent increasing as we slid further down. Then ahead and to my right I caught a glimpse of a ladder attached to the wall. Releasing the gun I made a grab for it, managing to hold onto one of the rungs while still struggling to get free of him. But he wasn't letting go. Instead, using me as a support, he scrambled to his feet.

'Who are you?' he panted, standing over me. 'Who are you to interfere in our affairs, the affairs of our nation?' He'd drawn a gun now and was staring down at me as I lay in the water, still clinging onto the foot of the ladder with one hand. It was a rhetorical question so I didn't bother explaining who I was, never mind why I was interfering in his mad schemes. He was standing close, leaning forward against the incline and the flow of the stream, his gun raised.

'He's dead,' I said. 'The code died with him. It's lost.'

Before he could respond I kicked out hard with my left foot, making contact with his knee. He had nothing to hold onto and staggered backwards, keeping his balance but only by wildly flailing his arms round. I got to my knees and with my full weight thrust forwards. Again we were tumbling, the gradient even steeper now, the water flowing fast, each of us trying to slow our descent, the enemy no longer each other, but the cascading waterfall. We were in a free fall, heading towards the light with no way to stop. We went over the edge of the culvert and plunged down into the river, each instinctively struggling to free himself from the other.

The first thing I saw when I came to the surface was a white-hulled river barge of the kind adapted for the tourist trade. It was no more than thirty feet away and beginning a turn from the Sava into the Danube at the confluence of the two rivers. I headed for the bank to get away from it, the throb of its engines and the churning of its propellers in the silty waters frighteningly close. I was getting pulled by the current, but falling behind the barge now, when I heard above it all a thin, high-pitched scream. I turned and looked back as he was swept into the slipstream and from there, as the scream stopped abruptly, into the propeller's suction. I could see passengers leaning over the stern rail. For a few seconds the barge's wake turned red, then back to the muddy brown it had been before. Yet spattered across the stern around the vessel's name, *Ruby Dawn,* were bright red streaks.

They'd soon get washed away, I thought as I struck out for the river bank.

Chapter 25

Piraeus, Greece

June–December 1999

In the months that followed, my life changed. I'd been at sea for nine years. Now I had to decide whether to make a proper career of it by qualifying as a deck officer, or to look for work ashore. I spent some time consciously reflecting on those years, looking back and remembering the best and worst of times to help me take a rational decision. But my mind was made up by an offer I couldn't refuse, and for which I had the Admiral, in part at least, to thank.

The Admiral took a keen interest in the affairs of the commercial shipping world, specifically when it came to maritime crime. While I had little knowledge of the inner workings of protection and indemnity insurance that shipowners took out to guard against calamity, I'd seen plenty of evidence of fraud, a number of serious and not so serious casualties, including those created purely to benefit from an insurance claim, and on one occasion, involvement in an attempted piracy attack, all of which had given me an insight into the risks involved in operating a fleet of merchant ships. Damage to cargo, engineroom fires and explosions or injury to crew and stevedores were worryingly commonplace too and from time to time, as a witness to such occurrences, I'd been called to give evidence along with ships' officers whose version of events often differed from my own. So in many ways the Admiral and I were on common ground.

When I finally returned to Piraeus, Christos Mavritis, who had generously recompensed me with full chief officer's wages and overtime allowance for the time I'd been away, took me to lunch at his favourite taverna.

'Maybe I can help you make your mind up. If you don't want to go back to sea, I can give you work here. Not full time, but enough to get you started. You know the business and I've seen you get involved in investigations and produce good reports. Your Admiral friend got in touch with me recently. He suggested I should talk to you about it. What do you think?'

I hadn't been expecting this. The prospect of another nine months on one of Christos's old bangers had little appeal. So without too much forethought I jumped at his offer. By the end of the year I had my own office in Notara Street, parallel to the vaunted shipowners' row, Akti Miaouli, and a short walk from the Mavritis offices. And I'd handled a variety of cases across the region: a cargo of Greek oranges that had gone rotten as the ship lay helplessly at anchor outside the frozen Sea of Azov; a fraught negotiation with a Croatian port manager who believed minor damage to one of his rusting old shore cranes was worth a million-dollar letter of guarantee with a substantial down payment because the ship, that he'd had arrested, had nudged the crane off its rails while berthing in high winds; and other incidents besides for Mavritis himself.

Very often these accidents and incidents were followed by a process of inquiry that could last for months or years. Surveyors and assessors from all the concerned parties would clamber over the ship inspecting damage, interviewing crew, port officials and stevedores, writing their reports and discussing the handling of the claim with the lawyers. I was now part of this circus and to my surprise, liking it. Such cases became my bread and butter, earning me considerably more than I'd have made at sea. And my fees were paid into an offshore dollar account in Cyprus.

But of more lasting importance was a meeting I'd had in the Edinburgh port of Leith with a protection and indemnity 'Club', the Caledonian Marine Mutual P&I Association. This venerable organisation insured the Mavritis fleet, and many others, against an assortment of risks. While they employed an array of agile-minded but office-based lawyers in Leith, they also relied on a network of freelance investigators and surveyors located in ports around the world.

Before I left their grand old building on Leith Links, I'd been signed up as one of their accredited correspondents, meaning I'd be handling cases involving Greek-owned ships entered in the Club as well as those involving their non-Greek tonnage, if and when they were involved in mishaps around the eastern Med.

Their American boss had been talking to the Admiral, who it seemed he'd known for many years, and having done the rounds in the office, I met him in the boardroom on the top floor where portraits of shipowners from the glory days of Scottish shipping and maritime enterprise graced the oak-panelled walls. Grant Douglas was an affable and expansive New Englander with a strong penchant for anything and everything Scottish, including his own Scots ancestry, which he explained to me in depth as we sat opposite each other across the oak boardroom table, that in itself must have weighed the best part of half a ton.

'You'll have gotten a pretty good idea of how we operate here so I won't go over it all again. I'd just like to give you a gentle warning. And it's something I explain to the folk here when they join, and remind them of on a regular basis. In the world of international shipping the rules are often blurred, so the oceans are pretty much lawless. And because of this, those who play for the highest stakes, be they owners, charterers, financiers or others, often do so with a sense of impunity. To them it's a sea of gold out there waiting to be mined. Keep it in mind, Angus. Because you'll meet them, and sooner or later, you'll come up against them.'

By early October I was feeling confident that the decision to set up my own business had been the right one. It was hard work and the flow of cases was uneven, at least in the early stages, but with my overheads under tight control and a generous payment from the Admiral for services rendered, I knew I'd survive.

I was standing on my balcony overlooking the Bay of Zea, or Pasa Limani as it was known in Ottoman days, reflecting on all this with the help of a whisky and as the sun set over Piraeus, when something on the TV news in the living room behind me caught my attention. I moved inside to watch the CNN report. It was showing two warships cutting through a choppy blue sea. The picture switched to a talking head reporting live from Beirut.

'Breaking news as a team of British Royal Navy Marines are reported to have boarded a merchant vessel some distance north of here as it was on its way to Beirut's port. A security blanket has been drawn over exactly what happened, but local sources have told CNN that the ship was believed to be carrying nothing less than a weapon of mass destruction, possibly a nuclear missile destined for an unnamed Islamic fundamentalist group. More reports as they come in …'

I phoned the Admiral to see if he knew anything about it. I hadn't heard from him since Belgrade, when he had reappeared and, along with Kirstin, taken care of Iveta. I had returned to Aleksandar's house in Zemun for a day or two while he was recovering, and from there flown to Athens.

Of course, he knew all about it. 'Well, there you are. Case closed, old boy!'

'You mean it was our Tochka?'

'Yes, of course. We sent an SBS team in last night as the ship approached the Lebanese coast. Same lot we used to rescue dear old Valdis in the Sulu Sea.'

'And what happened?'

'The vessel in question, the *Aegean Leader*, is now under escort from a couple of RN patrol boats, *Dasher* and *Pursuer*. The crew have been detained on board and a riding crew are manning her until she reaches the Akrotiri Mole in Cyprus. It's a secure berth within the RAF base there. The Tochka will be safely removed from there.'

'Have you told Iveta?'

'Yes. She knew all about it through the IAEA's Incident and Trafficking Department. But I understand the *Aegean Leader* is entered for P&I cover with your friends the Caledonian Marine Mutual. Her Greek owners, *prima facie*, are legitimate enough, but she's on long-term timecharter to a Georgian firm and they in turn have voyage-chartered her to a shadowy Russian outfit controlled, we suspect, by a group of ex-GRU agents, most probably the same rogue outfit you and Valdis came across in Latvia.'

'Why Beirut though?'

'Al-Qaeda is our best guess. They're increasingly active these days, you may have noticed.'

'You think they had a specific target in mind?'

'We don't know that. We do know the broker these Russians have been talking to. He's a Lebanese with a ships agency business. We suspect from our Beirut sources that he is, shall we say, sympathetic to the Al-Qaeda cause; certainly to the Wahhabi ideology. So for now we can only make an educated guess, but we're following it up. Meanwhile, you may wish to speak to Grant Douglas at the CMM. I understand you've met him haven't you?'

'Yes, I was over there recently. A fondness for all things Scottish.'

'I'd noticed that. He's just acquired some old pile in the Scottish Borders. He has the notion that his ancestors were reivers from that part of the world.'

The Admiral invited me to an island in the northern Aegean where he spent much of his time. I said I looked forward to it, but wanted to get the business established before taking time off. We agreed to stay in touch and rang off. I poured myself another whisky and went back onto the balcony. It was almost dark now and the lights glittered in the harbour from the ferries, gin palaces, yachts and, further out in the Saronic Gulf, the tankers, bulkers, bunker barges and workboats servicing the ships at anchor.

Next morning I phoned Grant Douglas. We discussed the case and I asked if they wanted me to get involved in the *Aegean Leader*'s case.

'Not at this stage,' he said. 'The owner hasn't paid his premiums. He says the charterer hasn't paid him charter hire for the past six months. Now the ship's in detention alongside at your British government's pleasure in Akrotiri. It's a goddamn mess but we'll let you know if we need your help. One way or another we'll be ditching the owner. Should never have taken them on in the first place but, hey, hindsight's a wonderful thing.'

So that was it. Or was it? What about the GRU gang who had brokered the deal as they had previously for the Black Hand? They'd failed twice now but that didn't mean they wouldn't keep trying. They were still out there, as were other loose nukes. I thought back to my days in prison with Valdis, of our perilous escape, of Vienna and Belgrade, Iveta and Aleksandar, and of the Surgeon's bloody end. Had it all really happened? But particularly I thought of Kirstin. We'd spoken regularly and she'd agreed to come down to Greece for a holiday. The Admiral had been pressing her to visit his island too.

***

It wasn't until a crisp, bright morning the day after Boxing Day that year that the Admiral called, just minutes after I'd arrived in my office. Making no reference to the events of the summer or our conversation in October, he asked whether I'd like to join him and some friends for the Millennium celebrations. I had no firm plans so accepted the invitation there and then. 'Where's it happening?' I asked, thinking he might be inviting me to his island.

'You'll see. Get yourself down to Limassol and they'll meet you at the airport. Just drop me a fax to let me know what flight you're on. Make sure you arrive on Thursday and I'll organise things from there.'

A few days later I came out of the terminal at Larnaca airport to be greeted by a uniformed driver who saluted sharply and took my bag. 'This way, sir, if you will.'

We walked out to where a Land Rover was parked, and with its RAF pennant fluttering, headed west towards the Akrotiri peninsula. At the airfield we drew up alongside a large, cumbersome-looking aircraft.

'What's that?'

'Boeing C17 Globemaster, sir. She's a long-range old bird but it's a long flight so you'll be refuelling at Ascension, I wouldn't wonder.'

'Where the hell am I going then?'

'Caribbean I heard, sir. But they don't tell the likes of me the specifics. It's all a bit hush-hush, I gather.'

I looked out of the window as we took off over the peninsula. There was a landing craft and the two fast-looking patrol boats alongside the mole, *Dasher* and *Pursuer* I assumed, but no sign of the *Aegean Leader*.

Chapter 26

The Caribbean

31 December 1999

As predicted by the RAF sergeant in Cyprus, the flight landed at Ascension Island in the middle of the Atlantic. The deceptively named Wideawake Airfield housing the RAF base on this burned-out volcano was strewn with potholes. Was that why it was so named, I wondered – to alert sleep-deprived pilots on the approach? We were on the ground there for an hour, refuelling and changing crew before heading west again. I dozed throughout the flight still wondering what I was doing travelling halfway round the world for a party.

'Welcome to Gitmo,' said another uniformed military man who greeted me as I came down the aircraft steps at my next stop. 'Here, let me take your bag. You came from Akrotiri, right? Tiring flight I guess.' He didn't wait for a reply. Instead he gave me a potted history of the base as we walked away from the plane. He'd introduced himself as Captain Dave Schlumberg of the United States Air Force. 'The rank is equivalent to an army colonel,' he told me, in case I needed to know. 'Got forty-five square miles of land and water here. Guantánamo Bay is on the south-eastern end of the island – Cuba that is. The US leased it to use as a coaling station and naval base back in 1903. Since the revolution here in '59, the Commie government has been protesting against our presence on their soil. They claim it's illegal and was forced on them. We call it a *fait accompli.*'

The midday sun burned down on my head and I could feel the heat thrown up from the tarmac through the soles of my shoes. I'd barely heard of this place, but the fact that we'd landed in Cuba reminded me of Valdis's experiences here during the missile crisis, and where he'd met his first love. But such thoughts were short-lived. We were walking across to where a helicopter crouched on the far side of the runway that we'd landed on.

'What now?' I asked still wondering why the Admiral had insisted on such secrecy.

'I'll see you over to the chopper. It's only a short ride.'

'To where?'

He laughed. 'Buddy, even if I knew I couldn't tell you. There are people on this base who would know, including the chopper pilot I hope, but I'm not one of them. It's the way it goes. But wherever it is, I guess you'll be there for the big Millennium bash, so enjoy yourself.' And as we reached the helicopter he handed me back my bag.

'You too,' I said and climbed on board.

It turned out to be a two hundred-mile flight which took us just over an hour and a half. 'If you're strapped in back there let's see if we can get this heap of shit airborne,' announced my pilot, who went on to inform me that, as we flew south-west out over the sparkling Caribbean, I was on board a Bell UH-1N Twin Huey and that this very aircraft had a history of flying special forces missions in Vietnam. That made it a very old aircraft. I wasn't reassured.

'Where are we headed?'

'Fucked if I know, man. I was just told to take you for a spin.'

When I didn't reply he laughed. 'Hey, lighten up buddy – chillax! We're headed for Jamaica. Yeah, man! You're one lucky sonofabitch. I love that island, man, and instead I'm stuck in Gitmo. It's a shithole I'm tellin' you. No booze, no chicks … well, almost.'

The monologue continued in the same vein until we crossed the Jamaican coast, when he decided to concentrate on where he was going. To my left I saw the forested slopes of the island's Blue Mountains, white beaches and clear turquoise waters. I was tired from the long flight and I was puzzled as to why the Admiral had chosen this place, but I couldn't help but feel faintly euphoric too.

We kept to the north coast heading west before putting down on a narrow strip of waste ground adjacent to the beach, with sand, dust and loose vegetation flying in all directions.

'This is where we say goodbye, man. You must be one important dude to justify all this secret squirrel stuff. You're a spook, right?'

I didn't answer. Was I a spook? Hardly. I'd only been dragged into the unholy mess by my resolve to help Valdis. It hadn't been a career choice.

Shielding my eyes from the dust storm and the blinding sun, I disembarked and, instinctively stooping, headed to where I saw a man waiting at the edge of the field. He was wearing dark glasses, dark blue chinos, a white short-sleeved shirt and a Panama hat which he was holding onto his head. He introduced himself as Sebastian but invited me to call him Seb. I let him take my bag and we walked over to his car, a black Ford.

'Where's the Admiral?' I asked, before getting in beside him.

'Oh, you'll be meeting him shortly. They're further round the coast. You'll like that part of the island – quiet, but there's plenty of nightlife not too far away.'

'Are you with the FCO here?'

'British High Commission, yep. Been out here a couple of years now. Love it. And tonight there'll be one hell of a party. I'll be in Kingston for that, but I've no doubt your Admiral will have something special planned too.'

We drove through small, unkempt settlements and minor traffic jams punctuated by frenzied overtaking and the incessant sounding of horns.

'How about yourself? I heard you were involved in some pretty hairy business in the Balkans recently.'

I turned to look at him. 'What do you know about that?'

'Sorry. Just an exchange I had with the Admiral and a friend of his I met the other day. I didn't mean to pry …'

'Are you a spook?'

'Heavens, no! It's a long time since Bond passed this way. Actually, you can visit Goldeneye if you have time. It's the other end of the island, but if you're going to be here for a few days I'd be happy to take you for a look-see.'

'I'll let you know. I'm not even sure what I'm doing here, but when the Admiral summons … I'm guessing it's not just about a Millennium party.'

The road turned south, taking us through the sprawling beach resort of Negril. To our right tourists and the odd Rastafarian hawker wandered along the beach while paragliders drifted overhead strapped into their harnesses beneath colourful sails lazily dragged along by motorboats below.

We passed a suburb called West End. 'See the lighthouse?' said Seb, pointing. 'That's where we're headed, just beyond it actually.'

Perched on a nearby clifftop I caught a glimpse of a bungalow amid a cluster of trees. We turned off into a drive and, after a couple of hundred yards, entered through a pair of new-looking iron gates.

The Admiral was standing by the front door, beaming. 'Good to see you,' I said, getting out of the car, 'but it's a long way to come for a party isn't it?'

'I know, I know, but how are you my boy? Long flight, eh? Had to have you over though. I've got some people I'd like you to meet.'

'Need me for anything else, sir?' asked Seb, addressing the Admiral. There wasn't, so we wished each other well for the Millennium and he turned the car and drove off to join his celebrations in the capital.

'So what's it all about?'

'Come with me and all will be made clear.'

The bungalow was from the colonial era and built before air conditioners became an everyday appliance. On this coast the breeze was almost constant, blowing gently through the whole house giving it an airy atmosphere. We walked through the hall and off to the right, where doors opened onto a veranda overlooking the bay, with the lighthouse visible a mile off to the north-west. Three people were seated on wicker chairs, talking. As we entered they all stood up. Two of the group were women: one small and dark skinned, the other was Iveta. But it wasn't the women I was staring at. For a second I thought only that the elderly man approaching me was vaguely familiar. But as he came closer, open-armed and smiling, despite his radically altered appearance, I knew it was Valdis.

We embraced. He was laughing but there were tears in his eyes, and in mine.

'What the hell …?' I was trying to process what and who I was looking at.

The Admiral spoke. 'Once we knew he was going to pull through we saw the opportunity to disappear him – keep him hidden from his enemies for good. Europe was not a safe place for him.'

'What have they done to you? You look twenty years younger! And why here?'

'Later. Now come,' said the Admiral. 'Tonight we will celebrate.'

I turned to Iveta. 'How long have you been here? Why didn't you tell me?'

'Sorry, but I was not allowed.' She cast a meaningful look at the Admiral.

'Angus, Iveta you know, but not Delfina.' So this was the old flame from his days in Cuba. We shook hands. I could see why Valdis had been attracted to her. She was in her late fifties and still a beautiful woman. Her long hair was greying yet her dark skin was lined only around the eyes, and then only when she smiled or laughed.

'He says you are the best friend he ever had,' she said.

'We have something in common then.'

'Yes, perhaps it is in the most difficult of times that the strongest bonds are formed.'

I looked again at Valdis. He didn't look twenty years younger at all. They had transformed him, but it had given his facial features an unnatural, slightly synthetic look. I'd noticed too his awkward walk when he'd approached me.

'Where did they do this?'

'A very private clinic in Switzerland. I was taken there from Serbia by air ambulance with the Admiral and Dr Kirstin. I was there for three months before I came here. Iveta was with me the whole time, after you found her.'

'Why Jamaica?'

'I would have gone myself to Cuba and looked for Delfina, but Admiral wanted somewhere he could keep eyes on me. Sebastian and good colleagues at High Commission have resources. I have one or two minders near me all the time. But I have things to tell you, when we're alone. We must make time.'

We ate and drank and talked, just the five of us. Initially I followed Valdis's advice and stuck to the Red Stripe. At midnight we watched a firework display up the coast. 'Rick's Café,' said Valdis. 'I'll take you to my bar near there. You will like it.'

Then the Admiral, not wanting to invoke too much merriment, said, 'Yes, Rick's Café. To be honest though, Angus, it wasn't just for the celebrations that I asked you over here.'

'I guessed that.'

'Well, you didn't have to accept my invitation.'

'I'm not sorry I did. But I knew when I got on that RAF plane, it wasn't just about a party.'

'Good. Tomorrow we'll get down to business then.'

The next morning, after only a few hours' sleep, the Admiral called us into the living room. The TV was tuned to CNN and he was eager we should watch as the rolling news stories were screened. He was clearly on edge.

'What's going on?' I asked, feeling the effects of sleep deprivation on top of too much champagne, which had somehow followed the Red Stripe from midnight onwards.

'Wait!' he said, turning up the volume. The headlines were all about the Millennium celebrations across the world and the ongoing debate over whether they'd got it all wrong and it was being held a year too early. There was little mention of the Millennium Bug which had failed to materialise it seemed. Instead it switched to a report from Moscow: 'News direct from the Kremlin this morning is that President Boris Yeltsin has resigned,' said the reporter. 'According to the constitution of Russia, Vladimir Putin has now become Acting President.'

The report continued with various self-proclaimed experts sharing their analysis of this purportedly unexpected event. In fact, it wasn't unexpected. Yeltsin's poor health and increasingly erratic behaviour, both due in some measure at least to his proclivity for alcohol, were no secret. Like a lot of Russians, Yeltsin considered beer a soft drink and instead favoured vodka, bourbon or red wine, or preferably all three at the same sitting. The writing had been on the wall for months. And Putin had already been appointed Acting Prime Minister by Yeltsin, who had publicly announced that he wanted him as his successor. Putin had earned a reputation as a tough law and order guy based on the way, as Prime Minister, he was dealing with the Chechen conflict. His previous career as a KGB officer was also common knowledge.

When the broadcast had finished, the Admiral switched the TV off and Valdis poured more coffee from a pot of local Blue Mountain. It was the best coffee I'd ever tasted. Delfina and Iveta were on the veranda, nursing their hangovers like the rest of us.

'You know,' said Valdis, who since I'd last talked to him, and now in secure retirement, had developed a tendency for lengthy discourses on any subject that came to hand, 'I remember in Byblos so many years ago my old friend Archie Anderson warn me that one day USSR would collapse. And it did collapse and it led to chaos. Things looked good for a while with Gorbachev, but Yeltsin has been a disaster, and now? What Archie said was that Russia would become like a Hydra. Monster unleashed from fall of Soviet state would grow many heads and totalitarianism would be replaced with what he called anarchic capitalism. There would be power-grab, corruption, cronyism: you cut off one head, two grow in its place. He was right. Where once there was KGB and GRU, now you have ex-officers from those services setting up on their own, or working for Mafia groups with oligarch bosses who grab state companies: oil and gas, mining, banking, yes, even rogue elements of military and intelligence agencies, all caused, and all grown by collapse of Communism.

'You know what Archie also said? That Cold War will not end with fall of Communism. There would be new Cold War. Why? Because Russia without mighty Soviet Union as protection against West would feel very vulnerable. And that will cause paranoia in its leaders. I believe Millennium will see new Cold War. Already we see these GRU guys buying nuclear weapons and selling on to highest bidder: Black Hand, Al-Qaeda, who next?'

'Which brings us nicely to the matter in hand,' the Admiral interrupted. 'Let's go back to our Tochka and the good ship *Aegean Leader,* loaded onto which was that very missile only a few short months ago. We brought both ship and missile into the harbour at Akrotiri, had the missile examined to confirm it was the same one that originated in the Zeltini base and found its way to the Golija mountains from where, as we know, it was transported back to Abkhazia. And indeed, it was armed with a one hundred kiloton nuclear warhead. This much you know, or will have guessed. What you don't know is that imprisoned on board the *Aegean Leader* in a small makeshift citadel, ostensibly installed to protect crewmembers against pirate attacks, was Colonel Fedir Oliynyk, a retired officer from the 37th Guards Rocket Division of Ukraine's 43rd Rocket Army. We took him ashore, fed him, then interrogated him. He talked freely, and for good reason. He had been abducted by a group of ex-GRU criminals whose intention was to coerce Oliynyk into arming the Tochka for them. Oliynyk had access to the PAL code and he had the knowledge to do this, but he had the motivation too, for they had abducted his twelve-year-old son and were holding the boy to ransom. Sadly, we learned the boy's body had been found with a bullet in his head, dumped by the road outside the city of Starokostiantyniv, not far from where Oliynyk lived and had worked. Bear in mind that Ukraine has been an independent state for the last nine years. Furthermore, since 1994 the country has agreed to destroy its Soviet nuclear weapons and join the Treaty on the Non-Proliferation of Nuclear Weapons. Clearly, this didn't deter our GRU boys, but when Oliynyk fell into our hands they saw no reason to keep the boy alive and in murdering him sent a gruesome message to anyone interfering with their nefarious activities. We must assume this is now their modus operandi, their business model if you like.

'We've handed the case over to Vauxhall Bridge but since shipping is their preferred mode of transport for moving these weapons around, the IMTF has an important role to play, an ongoing role.'

'So where do we go from here?' I asked. 'Not only can't you prevent these nukes falling into the wrong hands, but when they do, the bad guys – GRU or whoever – only need to identify the right man capable of accessing the PAL codes, then kidnap a family member as ransom.'

'Yes, that would seem to be the case. And in answer to your question – where do we go from here? – that is what we're here to discuss. Valdis has made it quite clear he wants to be involved. He knows that cannot mean a return to his field agent days. His proposal to me was that you, Angus, be appointed as his proxy in the field. I told him it was a splendid idea. I then took the liberty of having a quiet word with Grant Douglas. He was not averse to the idea either. He said it would be symbiotic. I believe we can make good use of you, but perhaps we can have your own thoughts?'

Which, I said, I was not ready to give him. I wanted to talk it through with Valdis first, and I recalled Grant Douglas's ominous warnings of lawless impunity on the high seas.

Early that evening we piled into two taxis and drove the few miles north to Rick's Café. Tourists and locals flock here at sunset to watch and try their hand at the cliff jumping. Every so often the lifeguard has a go from an even higher platform, and for this he expects a tip. The sunset was spectacular, which was more than could be said for the house punch they served. I was going to switch to Red Stripe when Valdis took my arm and spoke to the Admiral and the girls.

'Angus and I want to share drink for old times' sake. There's little bar I have down the road. I promised to take him there.' There wasn't much the Admiral could do about it. He'd become so used to 'running the show', as he put it, that to see Valdis neatly side-step him gave me a perverse pleasure. We left them to it and walked along the beach to Harry's Bar, where Valdis had befriended the barman. I noticed how Valdis walked with a heavy limp and even that short distance got him wheezing, but it didn't seem to affect his spirits.

Inside, there was the ubiquitous reggae playing – mostly Bob Marley or one of his offspring – and half a dozen customers gazing out at the sunset.

'Hey man, who's your friend? You both having the usual?' Harry had already begun mixing the drinks.

Valdis introduced us. 'Harry makes good Martinis. Now is good time for you. Try one. Remember, you will be meeting different kind of people now. Not like your shipmates. You must make changes: maybe pint in pub in the docks one night and Martini in luxury hotel bar next.'

'Okay, you've twisted my arm.' I was seeing a new side of Valdis: relaxed and expansive, despite everything he'd been through.

The drinks came. 'Thank you, Harry,' he said, then turning to me, 'Three ounces gin, half ounce vermouth – that is best, shaken in plenty of ice. But two is enough for me these days.' You can guess who introduced me to this habit.'

'Archie?'

'Yes, Archie. He was a great enthusiast.'

We raised our glasses and drank. He nodded towards the bar. 'Harry is not his real name. It's so he can call it Harry's Bar, just down road from Rick's Café!'

I took another sip. 'That's damn good, Valdis. But what was it you wanted to tell me? Was it about what happened on that bloody mountain?'

'No, I don't talk about that. With Iveta I have many conversations about our experiences. We must move on. Leave it behind.'

'Good. That sounds wise. Do you still remember the code?'

'Of course. But I tell no one: not Admiral, not Delfina or Iveta. And not you. Goes with me to grave. But of course, Oliynyk had it. There is always someone who has these codes in former USSR. But for me the code is special, sacred I think. More than just numbers and letters. When I took it I knew I was doing something important.'

'It was symbolic then.'

'Yes, for me code was not just a lock. It represent many things wrong in the world that must be stopped. Do you understand? That's why I wanted it, to keep it locked, in here.' He tapped his head.

'I understand, like a metaphor – it represents your moral code.'

'Yes, moral code. To stop killing of innocent people - everywhere.'

I'd never thought of it like that and I hadn't realised he had either. He shook his head as if to clear his mind of something that, for him, was already resolved, dealt with.

'I was going to tell you about Delfina.'

'She's lovely. You're a lucky man to have her with you after all this time.'

'I know this, although it is hard for me to forget what the British did.'

'What do you mean?'

He turned to look directly at me. 'Delfina was agent for British after we met. First for Naval Intelligence then later, when IMTF was formed, for them. She worked for MI6 too. She was full-time spy living all time in great danger for her life. GRU questioned her there in Cuba when investigating my case. She hated them. Vicious men, she said. Then she was talked to by local man. He was go-between. Introduced her to British case officer. First she was used to report ship movements in and out of Mariel port, then she visited other ports. She never had proper cover story. She was very good at talking her way out of difficult situations. It was for a college project she was working on; or she was visiting friends or relatives. She was a natural. After missile crisis and withdrawal of Soviet ships, she worked more for

MI6 than Naval Intelligence. That was very dangerous. She was spying on Cuban Politburo members. MI6 persuaded her to work as honey trap.'

'And she did?'

'Yes. Like me, she believed in a cause, against Communism.'

'So you lived parallel lives without knowing it. Did she ever marry?'

'No.'

'Was it Delfina who told Naval Intelligence about you after they recruited her? That you would make a good recruit too? That you could be turned?'

'Yes. It was her. Only now do I know this.'

He called Harry for another drink, then, smiling, he gripped my forearm. 'Imagine my surprise when she arrives here. Admiral arranged it. And once we had talked about it, of course we knew we had both lived not normal lives. Both done things we did not like to do. But when we had talked, and talked, we knew love was still there. We had only been together for one night. Now, so many years later, we knew we still had love.'

He paused. 'I wanted to tell you this story, because you know, Dr Kirstin was in Swiss clinic with me some of the time. She talked about you. She wanted to know everything.'

'And what did you tell her?'

He laughed. 'Of course, I told her everything!'

'I see. Well, I was planning to return via Scotland. I thought the Admiral might have invited her over here.'

'He did, but not possible. She had big family party at home in Scotland. You know, my friend, we've seen so many bad things, much pain and death. We must find love and happiness while we can.'

Harry brought the second round of Martinis across to where we were sitting. The sun had sunk below the sea now and we raised our glasses again.

'I agree. So to tomorrow then,' I said.

'Yes, and to peace.'

'And to peace. You know what Ronald Reagan said?'

'Yes, peace is not the absence of conflict, it is the ability to handle conflict by peaceful means.'

The End

In case you enjoyed *The Code*, I've included here the Prologue to *Sea of Gold*, where, two years after these events, Angus McKinnon takes up his story.

Sea Of Gold

'There is a tide in the affairs of men,
Which taken at the flood,
Leads on to fortune;
Omitted, all the voyage of their life
Is bound in shallows and in miseries.
On such a full sea are we now afloat,
And we must take the current when it serves,
Or lose our ventures.'
William Shakespeare, 'Julius Caesar', Act 4, Scene 3

Prologue

April 2002

Levan eased the car out from where he'd parked and sounded the horn to warn the young drunk weaving across our path in front of the airport. As we took off I caught sight of him in the wing mirror. Staggering, he flung the bottle towards us before fading away in our cloud of dust. The bottle shattered against the back of the car. It was eight-thirty in the morning.

'Welcome to Tbilisi,' said Levan as we drove away. We were heading north towards the city centre amidst commuter traffic and the occasional horse and cart.

'It reminds me of home,' I said to reassure him that early morning drunks were not exclusive to Georgia.

Levan glanced at me. 'You told me once that Greece was a café society. They're not big drinkers are they?'

'I was thinking of Scotland.'

'Ah! That's the weather. You drink to forget how miserable it is, eh?'

'Something like that.' I didn't want to get into a discussion about the Scots' drinking habits.

'You live in Greece, Angus. Isn't that home for you now?'

'I travel between the two but yes, I guess Greece is home.' The truth was I was not too sure where I belonged.

Georgia's roads weren't the finest example of civil engineering back in those days. We cleared the city and took the road to Poti, a three hundred kilometre obstacle course of potholes, some the size of small bomb craters. Perhaps that's what they were.

Levan flung the old Mercedes round them or just ploughed straight through. With no seat belt I braced myself, feet against the bulkhead between the foot-well and the engine.

'Relax will you,' he shouted above the noise from the engine. 'I drive down here every few weeks. I know this road like the palm of my hand.'

He lit a foul-smelling cigarette and swerved to avoid an old Soviet-era truck that was veering towards us.

'What are you laughing at?'

'It's a panic reaction,' I said. 'Anyway, you mean like the back of your hand.'

'No, like my palm,' he argued.

'Have it your own way, Levan. Tell me about these guys will you? You said they were from Ossetia. Which one, North or South?'

'For sure they're from Ossetia. Probably North. It doesn't make much difference.

'It might to me,' I said. 'I want to hear the whole story. And before we get to Poti.'

'My friend, it is complicated,' he began. Levan Beridze was a lawyer. He liked things complicated.

'When the good old USSR collapsed,' he began, 'the KGB left a few unexploded "devices" for us here in Georgia. They encouraged ethnic conflicts which had been festering for many years. They, how do you say it, stirred things up. They did this so they could justify keeping their military bases in our country to "assist" us in settling any outbreaks of ethnic unrest that they themselves were keeping warmed up. Ossetia was one of those time bombs.'

We were out of the city now, travelling through orchards and vineyards then, as we went further, through meadows carpeted with wildflowers. We passed hayricks and ragged boys herding goats. To our right the snowy peaks of the North Caucasus shone in the bright sunlight of early spring.

'Ossetia was always part of our homeland,' Levan said morosely. 'They took it from us.' The drooping moustache and dark patches under his eyes added to the sense of a man who had regrets about many things in life, but Levan was not a depressive. He was a jovial old bear. I remembered a time in Istanbul when we'd been at the same conference. In the evening, at a nightclub in Besiktas, he was the life and soul of the party; carousing and competing with the belly-dancers, singing Georgian folksongs over the bus's PA system on the way back to the hotel. The Georgians like to sing, and everyone liked Levan.

As I understood it, the Russians had established a strategic military platform in North Ossetia, a friendly neighbour in a troubled region they would argue, in order to control unruly breakaway republics in the North Caucasus which they considered were within their sphere of influence: enclaves like Chechnya, Ingushetia, Dagestan and Abkhazia. But I wasn't going to argue the politics with Levan. I was more concerned with the matter in hand.

Which was that a cargo of ethyl alcohol discharged from a ship called the *Med Runner* had been released from the port of Poti to a bunch of gangsters against production of false documents. If it had been that alone it would have been just another case for me, but it had become a whole lot more complicated when the Caledonian Marine Mutual P&I Association had, in its infinite wisdom, sent a rookie case-handler to Poti to deal with it. And the case-handler had failed to report back.

Grant Douglas was Chief Executive of the CMM, and he didn't phone often. The P&I Club, as such mutuals were known, offered shipowners protection and indemnity cover against third-party liabilities including claims for loss of cargo. As their correspondent in the East Med I didn't show up on Grant's radar much, but this was different and I sensed the anxiety in his normally urbane New England manner.

Why the hell did you send her, I'd asked. Surely he knew that pretty much all trade involving alcohol in these parts was controlled by violent criminal gangs?

'I made a judgement, Gus. That line's been trading in and out of Poti for a couple of years now and this is the first trouble they've had.'

'Sure, Grant, the Caucasus where as we all know business is conducted to the highest ethical standards and if you have a complaint you simply report it to the relevant authority on the requisite form and they will see to it straightaway.'

'Your sarcasm can be tiring. I know what these places are like but Claire was persuasive and finally we agreed it would be good experience for her to go.

'And anyway, these people must learn what it means to follow the rule of law if they want to do business with the West.'

I laughed. 'Really? I'll be sure to tell them that.'

Claire Scott was in her mid-twenties and considered a rising star in the CMM. For all I knew, she'd never been beyond the French Riviera, never mind to Georgia which, when all this blew up, was not the kind of place to send anyone on their first case.

Grant was unrepentant. 'We briefed her thoroughly. She knew she was to investigate the release of the cargo against fraudulent bills of lading, and no more than that. We made it clear to her that chasing down the crooks was not part of the brief. She knows the Club Rules as well as you and I do.'

'The shippers claimed against the line who, in this case are the ship's charterers. They passed it on to the owners who've passed it on to us. We'll negotiate with cargo underwriters and settle on the best terms we can manage, provided we're satisfied the master or his agent weren't complicit or negligent in releasing the cargo to the wrong consignee. You know how it works.'

He paused again. Then his voice hardened. 'Just go and get her out of there will you?'

And so it was that we were rattling along the road to Poti. Levan knew how these cases worked as well as Grant Douglas and I did – that Claire Scott's job had been to ascertain with reasonable certainty what had happened to the cargo, not to play cops and robbers. He'd taken her down this same road and left her in Poti just a week earlier, since when no one had heard a word from her.

'She was absolutely adamant she didn't want my help,' he said.

I had to wonder about that. 'Didn't you think to override her Levan? She's just a kid.'

'Have you met her?'

'No I haven't.'

'Well I tell you Angus, she is not one to be "overridden", as you put it. She is very self-confident – arrogant even, I would say. She told me she'd call me when she wished to return. I felt like I was her driver. So I left her to it.

'Anyway, it's not a war zone you know. Poti is a peaceful place. And I told her whatever she found out, not to pursue these people. They must have disappeared long ago up into the mountains. I warned her they would be armed and dangerous.' His voice trailed off as he realised the implications of what he'd just said.

The port, when we finally rolled in, was a scene of chaos. Containers were stacked five or six high on uneven waste ground. Antique forklifts and the odd creaking old reachstacker trundled around inside and outside the terminal's perimeter fencing. Trucks queued up the dusty road into the distance, engines running, black smoke billowing from their exhausts. Hungry-looking dogs, their coats patchy with mange, roamed the streets.

We started at the agent's office, a dilapidated building with a pale green exterior. It looked like mould growing up the walls rather than the intended finish. Perhaps years ago the architect and his builder had stood back to admire its post-Stalinist functional grace but I doubted it.

There were four people in the outer office. Levan asked to see Gia Nozadze and we were ushered through to a small glass cubicle in the corner. This part of the office was much like the rest except that it was adorned with a dirty grey carpet which was curling up at the edges.

Gia was a malnourished-looking character in his early twenties. His card announced that he was the branch manager. He looked nervous.

Levan introduced me and I began gently. The boy's English was poor so Levan translated to make my questions clear. Georgian was incomprehensible to me. Levan had said it was unlike any other language. Where else would the word for mother be *deda* and for father, *mama*?

'We want to hear from you about this case of the missing containers, and we want to know where Miss Scott is, the woman who came here last week.'

Gia took a file from a shelf behind him. I sat well back so he had to come round to my side of the desk to show it to me.

'Sit down,' I said, patting the chair in front of me. He sat.

I looked at the copy bills of lading covering the fifty-three forty-foot containers of ethyl alcohol shipped from Antwerp. They weren't bad as these kinds of forgeries go and I could almost believe him when he said he'd thought they were genuine.

The carrier's funnel markings showing the letters MBSCL and the name – Med Black Sea Container Line – were printed on the bill in what appeared to be their original design, font and colours. Other details of the shipment, including the ship's name and the cargo description, looked authentic enough.

'Tell me about the people who presented these to you,' I said.

They weren't consignees he'd seen before. They were well dressed. Five of them in two black BMWs. Nice cars.

'Their trucks were there too to collect the containers,' he said. 'The bills of lading looked okay so I issued the DO.'

They could present the Delivery Order at the port gate, collect the containers from inside the port and bingo, a million and a half dollars' worth of hooch was theirs. Only by the time it was turned into *cacha* vodka for the Russian black market it would be worth a good deal more.

'So how many trucks?'

'Two,' said Gia.

'Just two? And how long did it take them to remove all the containers?'

Two days he thought.

'So each truck was making twelve or more round trips a day,' I said. 'Allowing for loading and unloading there's no way they'd make it to North Ossetia, right? They'd get about thirty kilometres or so up the road at best.'

'To a yard or a warehouse or somewhere they could hold the containers or transfer what was in them,' Levan interjected. Gia shifted uncomfortably and looked at the floor.

I drew my chair closer to his. 'Levan, I want you to translate every word I say to our young friend here – slowly and carefully.

'Now listen hard. You're going to tell us everything you know about this little venture – who these people are, where they're offloading the containers and what they've done with Miss Scott. So get started, now.'

Levan translated but Gia answered sullenly in English. 'I know nothing. They came into this office. They presented the bills of lading. And then they left. That's all I know.'

I kicked the leg of his chair hard enough to make him jump. 'Not good enough. You tell us where the cargo was transferred or we will make it very hard for you. And we don't have much time, so make it quick.'

Levan translated again, up close to Gia's face, menacing him. I didn't much like this way of doing things but I needed information. We could take off up the road to Ossetia like the Keystone Cops and find nothing. I needed to know where they'd gone and Gia was my best bet right now.

Levan had grabbed hold of Gia's hair and was pulling his head around to get the point home. His resistance dissolved. 'They took the Zugdidi road. I don't know more than that. They said I shouldn't speak to anyone. They're mafia. They'll come back for me.'

'And the woman?'

'She met them. One of them who had come to the office came back in one of the trucks. She wanted to meet them. She went off in the truck. That's all I can tell you.'

Was she out of her mind? I turned to Levan. 'Zugdidi. How far?'

'Forty kilometres maybe, but my guess is we'll find them before that. There're a few places on the way where they could offload these boxes, Angus. Storage yards, old warehouses …'

We took Gia with us. He didn't want to come but I figured if we acted as if we'd forced him then the Ossetians, if that's what they were, might realise he'd been coerced rather than simply blown the whistle on them.

It didn't take us long. Half an hour from the port we saw the containers emblazoned with the line's livery, strewn across a bare patch of land a hundred metres or so off the road. Nearby was an old building, more a shack than a house. Levan stopped the car.

'Are you sure you want to do this, Angus? These guys aren't from your Salvation Army you know.'

I didn't see that we had a choice.

Several of the containers that had already been emptied were aligned into a block. I could see that the others were still closed with intact Customs seals on their doors.

As we approached a man came out from one of the containers. He was wearing a black leather jacket, sunglasses and carrying what I recognised as an AK-47 rifle. And he was big. Levan stopped the car ten metres in front of him. We got out and I walked towards the man.

'Hi! I'm Angus,' I shouted, giving him my most genuine warm and friendly smile. I held out my hand, which he ignored. 'We're looking for a colleague, a British woman. Have you seen her?'

Levan started talking to him in Georgian. I looked behind them to the interior of the containers. One had a white plastic table and chairs placed just inside its doors.

Another was being used to store what looked like cartons of food and bottled water. Inside the third container a small portable generator was running. It looked like a makeshift workshop.

'He says this is private property and we should leave,' Levan translated. 'He says he hasn't seen any woman.'

'Okay,' I said, 'he won't mind if we just have a quick look around then will he.'

I moved towards the container with the table and chairs. The man stepped across my path.

I raised my arms in a gesture of reassurance and smiled. 'It's okay, Ivan. I just want to have a quick look.'

'*Nyet!*' he said and pushed me backwards. I stumbled but regained my balance before I fell.

He spoke to Levan.

'He's telling us to get out, Angus.' Levan sounded anxious.

'We need to look, Levan. What's he so worried about? Tell him we're not interested in the cargo, just the girl.'

Again Levan translated but it did nothing to placate the man.

I stepped towards him. He raised his rifle. From the way he held it I was reasonably sure he was going to strike me with the butt. With my arms open in what I hoped looked like a conciliatory gesture I lifted my right foot and brought it diagonally across and down onto his left ankle, heavily, pulling his rifle away from him as I did so.

The human foot and ankle together form a complex mechanism consisting of some twenty-six bones, thirty-three joints and over a hundred muscles, tendons and ligaments. The sound of this lot crushing beneath my boot came before the scream. Ivan went down grabbing at his ankle, the scream turning to a bellow of fury.

It had happened in seconds. Keeping hold of the gun I turned to Levan and Gia. They were staring aghast, frozen to the spot.

'Keep an eye on him while I look around, okay?' My voice trembled as I spoke. I was shaken but I was committed now and I didn't want us hanging around there longer than necessary.

I was about to step into the first container when I heard a shout. It came from the furthermost container. I ran over to it and into the back of the forty-foot steel box. They'd got her locked in a makeshift cage. A mesh of steel reinforcing bars had been cut to size and welded across the width and height of the container. A section a metre high and less than half a metre across had been cut out then repositioned and held in place with four heavy padlocks – two on either side.

'Hang on,' I said and returned to where Levan and Gia were standing over Ivan. I guessed the keys to the padlocks would be in his pocket and reached down to get them. We exchanged looks. His face was contorted with pain. He didn't look happy. I took the keys and went back to let the girl out.

'You're Claire, I take it,' I said superfluously as I unlocked two of the padlocks and pulled the mesh open. There was an old mattress, a table and chair and some bottles of water inside the cage. On the table was the remains of what looked like the *khashi* soup Levan had been telling me I should try. It didn't look at all appetising.

'Yes, and you are?' Any thought that she'd fall gratefully into my arms was quickly dispelled. Claire Scott defied assumptions.

'Grant Douglas asked me to find you. We now need to get out of here before Ivan there or his pals decide otherwise.'

She hesitated so I grabbed her arm and marched her towards the car.

'Levan, we're leaving now.'

'Wait!' the girl shouted. She pulled away and ran back to the container.

'Get the car turned round, Levan,' I said and went back after her. She had found her handbag into which she was stuffing papers lying on a table near the container's doors. 'I'm not leaving without these,' she said defiantly.

She was a little dishevelled-looking but considering she'd been held captive for a couple of days at least I guessed, she didn't seem too much the worse for wear.

I went searching for something to constrain Ivan with and found a coil of rope in the container which was being used as a workshop. We trussed him up as best we could. He wasn't putting up much resistance.

Then I grabbed hold of young Gia by his jacket, shook him hard and pushed him to the ground. 'As for you, you little shit, don't think we don't know you're in on this.' Levan caught on and reiterated the message in his native tongue. I hauled Gia up and propelled him towards the car, the little charade being for Ivan's benefit. He was lying on the ground gaping at us. I didn't want him thinking Gia was our accomplice, for Gia's sake.

Levan drove like the wind - that is to say in his normal manner. We dropped Gia off near his office in the port. He was agitated. He told Levan he was going into hiding. I passed him the gun I'd taken off Ivan for which he seemed grateful. Then we picked up the road back to Tbilisi.

'Levan,' I said. 'Call your office and tell them to book us seats back to Istanbul on tonight's flight will you?'

'Sure. We'll head straight for the airport,' he said punching in a number on his phone.

Claire Scott was looking at me. We were both in the back of the car. 'Well aren't you just the all-action hero then. Do you make a habit of crippling people when you first meet them?'

'Look,' I said. 'I'm sorry if I disturbed your cosy little moment with Ivan back there but it didn't look like he was about to start serving you afternoon tea. Or am I missing something?'

'I'm sorry,' she said without much conviction. 'I do appreciate you coming to the rescue, really.' She was examining herself in a small mirror she'd fished out of her handbag. She began wiping her face with a cleansing tissue.

'My bag's back in the hotel, bugger it.'

'You'll just have to manage I'm afraid. Maybe we can get you something at the airport.'

She was slightly built with dark hair which she'd tied back into a ponytail. Wide cheekbones, eyebrows that swept upwards slightly, clear grey eyes and flawless skin.

'Were you mistreated?' I asked. 'It wasn't exactly the Ritz they had you in back there.'

'No I wasn't. I was getting lecherous looks though. They let me wash. There was a bathroom of sorts. It was disgusting.'

The drive back seemed to take forever although Levan flogged the old Merc to its limit. I just hoped it would last the journey. I didn't ask Claire what she'd thought she was doing playing at Lara Croft. That could wait.

Levan's office had got us seats on Turkish Airlines' evening flight. We had time but I was worried about Levan and said so. He'd spotted a couple of black BMWs behind us as we were approaching the Tbilisi suburbs. They were keeping their distance but if it was our gang then they must have travelled fast to catch up with us.

'Don't worry Angus,' he replied cheerfully. 'They're cheap crooks. Their interest is in getting that ethanol up to North Ossetia, turning it into bootleg vodka and selling it into Russia on the black market. They're not interested in me or you.'

'I wish I shared your optimism,' I said.

We reached the airport and Levan pulled in to drop us off. Almost immediately the two BMWs were there, one in front, one behind us. Four men came towards our car, two from the front and two from the rear. They were all wearing black leather coats and dark glasses like it was their uniform. Behind them was another man wearing a long, expensive-looking grey coat with a black fur collar, and no shades. One of the thugs yanked open Levan's door and gestured for him to get out. Grey Coat, flanked by two of his goons, stood with his arms folded. He spoke to Levan for a few moments, everything nice and calm. Levan came back to my side of the car. I wound down the window, about an inch.

'It's okay, Angus. He wants to talk to you, that's all.'

'Really, well that's reassuring.'

'Stay put,' said Claire. I got out and walked with Levan to where Grey Coat was standing, arms still folded. We looked each other up and down. He was in his early fifties I guessed, medium height, thin and ascetic-looking. His grey hair was swept back from his forehead and he sported a Lenin-style goatee beard and moustache. It was a sharp, angular face with a hooked nose. And dark, piercing eyes that never left mine for a second.

'Hi,' I said.

'Listen, English.' He spoke slowly, his voice soft and guttural. 'You and your woman went a step too far back there, you know? You keep your nose out of my business and I don't trouble you, okay? You ever come back here, you never leave. Understand?

'I will let "Ivan" do what he wants with you – and it'll be very bad if you ever call him that again. He'll break more than just your foot after what you did to him.' He was prodding me in the chest now. I took it to be a threat.

'Yes, sorry about that, my foot slipped. But listen to me, pal,' I said. 'If you're responsible for the theft of that cargo then sooner or later the forces of law and order will catch up with you. Maybe not me, or this guy,' I gestured to Levan, 'but sooner or later they'll get you. Don't imagine your Procurator Fiscal doesn't know about this case. And remember, when you point a finger at someone like that, three fingers are pointing straight back at yourself.'

I walked back to the car and got in. I looked back. Levan was talking to Grey Coat, waving his arms around in an effort to placate him I sensed.

'For God's sake, are you crazy?' Claire exploded. She'd wound the window down and listened to the exchange. 'They could have shot you there and then.'

'I didn't want them thinking they could just intimidate us with impunity like that. Levan has to live and work here, remember?'

'I just hope you haven't made matters worse, that's all.'

'Well without labouring the point, who the hell got us into this in the first place?'

Levan returned to the car.

'Well?' I said.

'It's okay I think, but Angus you shouldn't have done that. The guy's a big cheese in these parts. He has *blat*.' It was an all-purpose Russian word for influence and corruption. 'And by the way, his name's not "pal", it's Boris Kaliyagin. He's, how would you say, a lesser oligarch but with many fingers in many pies. Not just the *cacha* market, other things too. He's from Svaneti in the north and they say he controls the illegal gold prospecting business there. And he just said he can stop your plane departing if he wishes. He said to tell you this.'

'Oh? And how would he do that?'

'He has the franchise on the fuel supply to all planes flying out of this airport. Believe me, he can.'

***

Istanbul. A city I never tired of, until now. We'd gained two hours on the flight back from Tbilisi, but I was weary and that evening Claire Scott and I headed straight for the hotel Levan's office had booked for us.

I needed a drink. 'I'll be in the bar if you want to join me for a nightcap,' I told her as we checked in.

'I'll be down,' she said and went up to her room to change.

I ordered a large Scotch and slumped into a leather armchair in a corner of the dimly lit bar. I was beginning to relax.

Claire appeared when I was well into my second drink.

'Wow! That's quite an outfit.'

'Spare me the sarcasm. It's all I could get in the hotel shop here. The one I was wearing was ruined.'

She'd put on a silky black cocktail dress. She looked wonderful.

'I meant it.'

She smiled as if she knew I didn't. I'd never understand women's take on fashion. I guess the dress was out of style or something, but it still looked great on her. Anything would.

The waiter was hovering over us before she even sat down. She ordered a Scotch, downed half of it as soon as it arrived and asked him for another.

I decided to get to the point. 'We can do this now or tomorrow but I need to ask you what in the name of God you thought you were doing back there, following those heavies. You could have got yourself killed and that's not the kind of risk we're expected to take. Didn't they tell you the limits of the investigation when they briefed you back in Leith?'

'I might have got a bit carried away,' she said without conceding that she'd screwed up. 'I thought if I could find the chief guy I could at least interview him. And that would strengthen our own defence when it came to negotiating a settlement with cargo underwriters.'

'That's true. But how about the legitimate consignee in Georgia? Did you talk to him?'

'I tried to find him through Gia, the agent, but his office said he was travelling.'

'My guess is he was mixed up in the whole scam,' I said. 'Think about it. It would be a win–win for him. He'd benefit from the black market sale of the *cacha* and recover the value of the ethyl alcohol from his cargo insurers too.'

She looked at me. 'You think I'm a fool don't you.'

'Not at all. A little naïve perhaps.' I was finding it difficult to maintain my frustration with her.

'It was foolish. But I knew I could talk my way out of it once Boris the boss man arrived. You saw at the airport. He didn't want any more trouble. He just wanted us off his back.'

She paused. 'Anyway, it's such an adrenaline rush.' She was high-spirited all right.

I sighed. 'Okay, I know what you mean. I get carried away myself sometimes, but learn from this. I mean it.'

'I will, honestly,' she said contritely. I wasn't convinced.

'How did you get into this game yourself then, Angus?' she asked.

'By accident.'

'What, you fell over a claim you mean?' Shc had a smile that was both mocking and inviting.

'Very funny,' I said and ordered more drinks.

‘I was working on a Greek ship. I wanted to come ashore. The owner offered me work in his claims department.’

‘Working on a Greek ship?’

‘I was an able seaman, then bosun.’

‘I thought those jobs went to Filipinos.’

‘Often they do. But this owner liked to mix his crews and in my case I was looking for some travel and a bit of adventure, not a career.’

‘So we’re not unalike, you and me: looking for something different to do with our lives.’

‘I guess so. It was a while back.’

She sat up and pushed her glass away. ‘Fancy a quick spin in the nightclub downstairs?’ She saw me hesitate. I’d drunk three whiskies and they weren’t British measures.

‘Come on!’ she insisted.

‘I’m not a Whirling Dervish you know. I can’t spin. I can’t even dance.’

She giggled. We went down anyway.

When I woke next morning sunlight was seeping through a gap between the curtains. I looked down at her asleep beside me. After a while she opened her eyes.

‘Good morning,’ she murmured, reaching her arms up and pulling me towards her.

ABOUT THE AUTHOR

Nick Elliott began his career as a boarding agent attending ships in Edinburgh's port of Leith. He moved to Hong Kong in the seventies and lived throughout the Far East for twenty years before relocating to Greece and eventually back to the UK.

Married with two daughters, he divides his time between Scotland and Greece.

ACKNOWLEDGEMENTS

My thanks to my ever-tolerant and diligent editor, Helen Bleck; to old friend from Hong Kong days and my enthusiastic beta reader, Andrew Watson; and to my wife Liz for her occasional but always well-judged suggestions. With their patient and good-natured encouragement they have helped immensely in ensuring *The Code* completed its journey.

Thanks also to Doctor Jane Stanford, Rear Admiral (ret'd) Roger Lockwood, Steve Cameron and Jeremy Waller for their expert input throughout the series. Also to author friends, Craig Russell and Peter A. Flannery for their ongoing advice and support.

And I am indebted to Ben Macintyre for his superb account of Kim Philby's defection in A Spy among Friends which helped to set me on course.

IF YOU ENJOYED THIS BOOK

If you enjoyed reading *The Code* I would be very grateful if you would leave a short review, or failing that a rating, on Amazon. Good reviews and ratings help other readers find and enjoy a book.

And if you would like to receive my newsletter, please go to my website: https://www.nickelliott.org or get in touch direct by email at nick@n-elliott.co.uk

Nick Elliott

SEA OF GOLD, DARK OCEAN AND BLACK REEF

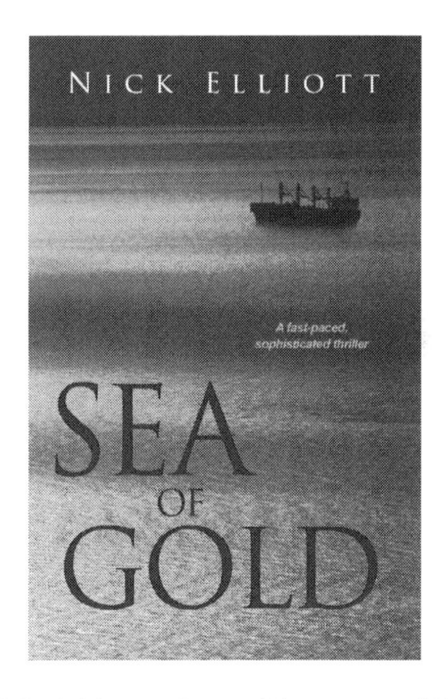

Buy Sea of Gold here: http://amzn.to/1jkQUYT

What readers have said about Sea of Gold

"Nick Elliott ticks all the boxes in this fast-paced yarn, with a keen eye for descriptive detail and solidly drawn characters. The first-person narrative, complete with ironic internal asides, is the perfect vehicle for a thoughtful and witty style that draws us swiftly into the shoes of its protagonist, a credible and consistent character."

***

"A unique twist on the spy detective thriller featuring impeccably researched action that is set in a host of well invoked locations. I look forward with intrigue to Angus McKinnon's further adventures."

***

"This is a first rate, well-constructed first novel which benefits from the author's learned insight into the maritime business world and his familiarity with interesting parts of the world. In addition he introduces us to some interesting characters who fortunately survive the tricky circumstances in which they find themselves and who we look forward to meeting again in the sequel(s). I predict a successful future for Nick Elliott who will I feel sure continue to set his stories in fascinating parts of the world. I thoroughly enjoyed this book."

***

"In the tradition of Eric Ambler, this is a well written crime novel. What starts out as a case of insurance fraud turns into a battle of international intrigue."

***

"A fascinating and very well-written story in a world I knew nothing about, commercial shipping. If you are a mystery fan, enjoy reading about international intrigue, appreciate well-developed complex characters and are curious about or fascinated by the high seas, this is for you. A powerful first book."

Buy Dark Ocean here: http://amzn.to/2vIPRyJ

What readers have said about Dark Ocean

"This really is an expertly researched, very well-written and fast-paced international thriller. The protagonist, Angus McKinnon, is a character with real dimension and credibility, which is something often lacking in this kind of fiction. You believe in him, and you believe in the streets, alleys and seaways he travels: every location is atmospherically and authentically created as your drawn deeper and deeper into a dark world where nothing is what is seems. Superb book."

***

"Felt like I was back in the Orient when I was reading this book. I could easily visualize every aspect of the author's descriptions of people and places. So many plot twists. Thoroughly enjoyed this book."

***

"Dark Ocean hit landmarks with which I am familiar (Kowloon and Hong Kong), and I loved all the interesting tidbits of shipping detail, description of ports, and customs of the locals, including the exchange of commerce with Japan. This book grabs your attention immediately then quickly widens to that of international intrigue that includes the collusion of a major cabal in what might be a hostile takeover--a far-reaching takeover. The threatening organization is deeply rooted and far ranging and has Angus flying to retrieve information from sources he thought well buried in his past--only to have to retrieve, relive, and sort. But as with any good thriller, a piece of the puzzle only leads to hints of acquiring the next piece.

***

"The book is a well-plotted, multi-layered suspense with slightly rogue alpha male management style being ever more deeply entangled in MI6 as they coordinate between agencies. There is so much (fictional?) information here reading as gospel that it becomes scary."

***

"Nick Elliott has done it again. Following Sea of Gold he has come up with an equally gripping, intelligent and well-paced thriller in Dark Ocean. Set in the shipping industry which he knows intimately and in countries which he knows like a native and in which you can feel the pulse of the street life, the plot leads you on in an unputdownable way. Once started you have to read on to the end. The characters, especially the female ones, are excellently crafted and true to life. Who knew that shipping could be so interesting?"

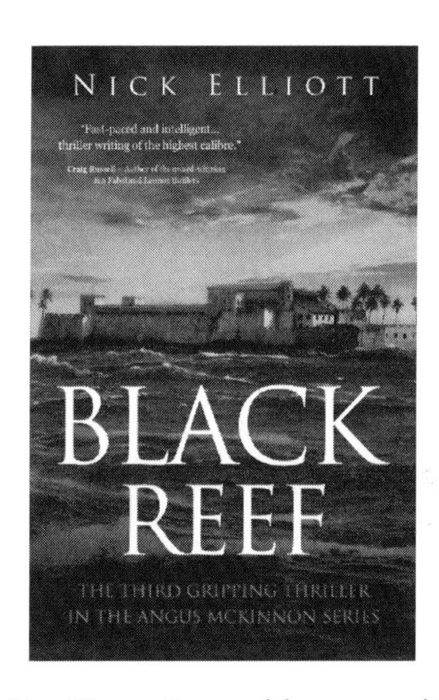

Buy Black Reef here: https://amzn.to/2zVBo4e

What readers have said about Black Reef

"I have now completed the Angus McKinnon trilogy and they get better and better. Like the previous two, Black Reef covers a tremendously wide geographical canvas written with Nick Elliott's intimate knowledge of those parts of the world together with the people who live there. So the book is fascinating on that count alone; add the breadth of the story, the excitement and suspense at almost every page and the quality of the writing and you have an action thriller amongst the very best. This book stands alone from the previous two, but if you haven't read them yet - do!"

***

"Nick Elliott does it again, his work just gets better and better. If you have read Nick's first two books this is a must read. If you haven't read the others then you have three must read books to enjoy. Can't wait for the next one."

***

"I really enjoyed meeting Angus again and being drawn into this third thrilling case. What a great trilogy. I particularly enjoy the depth of knowledge Nick Elliott shows when it comes to the different locations Angus finds himself in, as well as the fascinating mysteries of the shipping world. What great reads!"

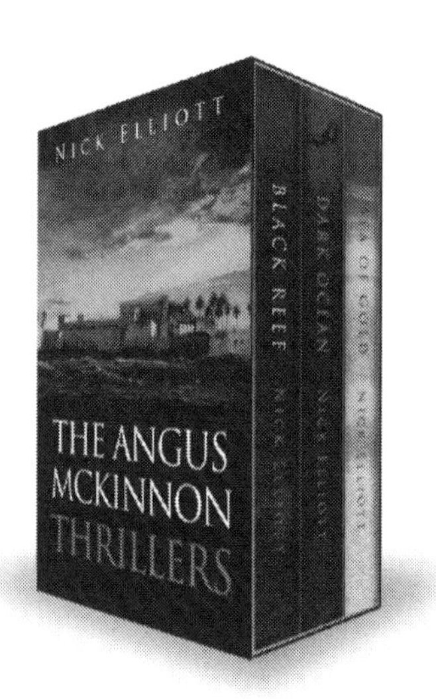

Or buy the trilogy box set here:
https://amzn.to/2Ov8WhE

Printed in Great Britain
by Amazon